# Having It All

Larissa Johns

Published by Larissa Johns, 2020.

This is a work of fiction. Similarities to real people, places, or events are entirely coincidental.

HAVING IT ALL

**First edition. December 10, 2020.**

Copyright © 2020 Larissa Johns.

Written by Larissa Johns.

To my parents, Sandra and Noel, for your ongoing
love and support. Thank you for everything!

# Prologue: Ten Years Ago

I t was my fellow Year 1 teacher, a friendly but somehow intimidating woman in her 50s, who first asked me when I got "the call" to teach.

Embarrassingly, I thought she meant the literal phone call offering me a job, and I responded accordingly. "No, no," she said, laughing. "I mean when you got *the call*. When you knew it was the right thing for you."

That's when I knew I was in trouble.

Growing up, I had no doubt that I would be a mum someday. I was five years old when my younger sister Julie came along, and I loved treating her as my own living doll. I was only about 13 when I started brainstorming baby names, usually overly feminine ones for the three girls I imagined I'd have. One thing I never expected to be was a teacher. I had romantic notions of being a writer, balancing babies on one arm while I frowned, pen behind my ear, at my manuscript, drafting bestselling novels. Reality had its way with me, as it always does, and after two years of travelling between school and uni, I had finally realised that I wasn't becoming a novelist at 20, and had decided to study teaching instead. It was a smarter way to use my time, and at least this way I could pass on my love of reading and writing to a new generation. So here I was, 24 years old and feeling ancient, getting started on my teaching career. In basic terms, I still hadn't received 'the call'. I was teaching because it felt safer than my other options, even though I had realised through my field experiences while I was studying that it wasn't all that safe, after all. I was teaching because I didn't know what else to do. It was terrifying.

"Come on," my teaching partner – Rosemary – said, perhaps sensing that she'd stressed me out. "Let's head over to the staffroom and I'll introduce you to people."

We went to the staffroom and, as promised, Rosemary introduced me to dozens of people whose names I couldn't hope to remember, at least not without staring at their chests to see their nametags, which didn't seem particularly preferable to just asking their names. The last person she got to was a young blonde girl, looking as ghostly pale and nervous as I felt. "You must be Carrie?" Rosemary asked. "I'm Rosemary, this is Annabel. She's a first-year, like you."

"Everyone calls me Annie," I said, smiling at Carrie. "What grade do you have?"

"Grade Five," Carrie said faintly. "I've only taught lower grades in my pracs, and I'm early childhood trained, and I really don't know why they've given me Grade Five! It was a bit of a shock, obviously." She stopped abruptly, as if worried she'd said too much, giving herself away.

"Oh, that's hard," I said sympathetically, suddenly not eager to tell the other graduate that I had been given Year One – although of course she asked, and I told her, and I saw the wistful look in her eyes. I also decided to keep the fact that I wasn't, in fact, early childhood trained to myself. I'd only received the job offer late, probably after they'd already appointed Carrie to Year Five, and I didn't see the point of rubbing it in.

By unspoken agreement, Carrie and I ended up sitting together for the Professional Development session; two clueless, anxious graduates against the world. Neither of us spoke much (uncharacteristic for me, but I'd never felt so nervous in my life) but there seemed to be a nice sense of camaraderie in sharing the experience with each other, rather than sitting with some of our more experienced co-workers.

At lunchtime we started to talk more, standing around in the staffroom with plastic plates full of the nibbles the Principal had provided for the first day back. I noticed a sign that said "please put your plate's in the dishwasher _**before**_ leaving the staffroom!", with 'before' italicised, bolded _and_ underlined, which seemed like a bit of an overstatement. "My God," I said to Carrie, pointing at the sign. "There's an incorrect apostrophe. On a sign made by teachers. This is disgusting. Besides, you can't load the dishwasher _after_ you leave the staffroom!"

"Wow," Carrie said. "My father would be spinning in his grave." She paused, looking momentarily surprised at her own statement. "Of course, he's not actually dead. He's in Taringa. But he wouldn't be happy, anyway."

I laughed, taken aback by her comment. Something about her dry delivery, her slightly politically incorrect statement, endeared me to Carrie. We continued chatting away and by the end of the day, I felt like I'd known her forever.

THE PROFESSIONAL DEVELOPMENT days came and went, and pretty soon I was staring down the barrel of my first day with my own class. It was a surreal feeling. Maybe I'd used up my year's supply of nervous energy by then, but I actually felt a strange sense of calm when I stood in front of them for the first time, and the day went well. My students seemed pretty sweet, all things considered, and it was a surprise to realise I actually really enjoyed what I was doing. Teaching without a supervising teacher staring over your shoulder, always ready to judge you, was much more enjoyable, and I felt more confident in my own abilities.

It wasn't until the Friday night, though, that it really sunk in how much I was enjoying my new profession. I had my friend Cherie's birthday drinks in the Valley, where I knew exactly no one aside from the birthday girl. I quickly found that when people started talking to me all I wanted to do was tell them what I did for a living, or fill them in on little stories about the kids in my class. It was a nice realisation, although I'm not sure it endeared me much to Cherie's hairdresser friends. I noticed most of their eyes glazing over when I started in on my new job with too much detail, and most of them quickly found an excuse to head off and talk to someone else. No doubt, someone with more interesting stories to share!

Half an hour in, I was sitting at the bar, half-perched on a bar stool with one leg extended to the bar at the bottom of the stool, feeling pretty out of my depths. I'd always hated being at parties where I didn't know anyone – small talk got old pretty quickly, and Cherie's friends mostly all knew each other already. I was extroverted to a point, but I wasn't about to muscle in on people's conversations. So I ordered cocktail after cocktail and tried to look the part of someone who was having a good time; or at least, someone who wasn't secretly daydreaming about being home in bed. Teaching might have been fun and it might have been my newfound passion and all the rest, but it was *exhausting*.

That's when I first saw Jack Delaney. He was immediately eye-catching, with dark curly hair, deep blue eyes (oh, how I love the combination of dark hair and light eyes!), and an ever-so-slightly devilish grin.

When Jack came towards us, the night instantly improved, my mood lifting. "Happy birthday, Cher!" he exclaimed, grabbing Cherie enthusiastically around the waist. "You look amazing. Having a good night?"

"Better now that you're here, Jackie," Cherie laughed, kissing him on the cheek. "Been a while. How have you been? Oh, Jack, this is Annie," she added casually, gesturing in my direction, possibly sensing me staring.

"Hi, Annie," Jack responded with an easy smile, which alone was enough to quicken my heart rate. "Hey," I replied breathlessly, trying to sound calm. Suddenly simple statements such as "it's nice to meet you" or "how do you know Cherie?" were far beyond me. I was, quite simply, captivated. It was a new feeling for me, but it was definitely there.

Cherie saw some newcomers and ran off, leaving Jack alone with me at the bar. "Do you know anyone else here?" I asked, finally regaining the power of speech.

"No, just Cherie. Well, and you, now. How about yourself?"

"Same here," I said, trying to ignore the thrill that ran up my spine. This guy was not only gorgeous, he seemed really sweet. "Should we -?" I gestured to some low black leather armchairs that sat away from the crowd, and Jack nodded. "Lead the way." We proceeded to chat all night, and I walked away feeling like I was floating on a cloud.

I didn't realise it at the time, but that's how I met two of the most important people in my life, one week apart.

# Chapter 1: Present Day

"Oh Romeo, Romeo!" Carrie called over the balcony, her voice a high falsetto.

I glanced up at her, shielding my eyes from the sun. "What's up, Juliet?"

"I need you, my love, my hero." She dropped the falsetto and used her natural voice. "You need to come help me move my damn desk."

"Oh, for the love of God, Caz," I grumbled, making my way up the stairs to her classroom. "How often do you have to re-arrange your classroom?" Carrie and I were alike in many ways when it came to our teaching style, but she did care a lot more about the appearance of her classroom than I did. My basic principle was, if the kids were being educated and no one was at immediate risk of electrocution, did it really matter if the room itself was spotless?

"At least once a month as always, my peach," Carrie cooed. "Now get over here." She was standing on one side of her desk, already poised to push it. "We're going over there." Together we slid the desk over to the other side of the room, with no small amount of effort.

We were both breathing pretty heavily by the time we stopped. Teacher desks weren't light but even so, it was fairly obvious we'd both neglected our fitness in recent years. Neither of us were tiny when we'd met in our 20s, but we'd essentially become anecdotal evidence of the 30-something spread. For Carrie's part, of course, childbirth had played a part, whereas for me, it was more about great Italian food and an overwhelming lack of desire to go to the gym with anything approaching regularity. When there were so many things to watch on Netflix, surely exercise was an overrated and much less appealing alternative?

We did talk, with our friend Georgia, about the idea of working together to eat well and exercise more, but when the three of us actually got together it more regularly devolved into giggling our way through drive-thru queues or seeing who could eat the most Maltesers in the shortest possible time. It wasn't healthy, but it was fun.

"So I see you two are cheating on me," said a sardonic voice from the doorway. We turned to see Georgia, as if I'd summoned her with my thoughts. I gestured towards Carrie's room-organising operation and said "you're more than welcome to take over. You two can cheat on me for a while instead." I sighed with exaggerated exhaustion.

Georgia seemed to consider this for a moment, then said "on second thoughts, you can keep on cheating."

"You're both hilarious," Carrie said, rolling her eyes. "I'm finished, anyway. You can both quit your bitching." When the three of us were together two always seemed to end up ganging up on the other, but we all knew it was light-hearted. Carrie and I had worked well as a duo for several years before Georgia started at our school four years earlier, and Georgia had fitted in as neatly as a missing puzzle piece we hadn't even realised we'd needed. It felt like we'd all known each other for decades.

Ten years ago I never would have imagined that Carrie and I would still be at Fallen Oaks Primary, or that we'd still be working together. It was a well-known statistic that a huge percentage of teachers quit the profession entirely within the first five years, so both of us still being teachers was unusual enough, let alone staying at the same school. Our enduring closeness was unusual as well, it seemed. I'd heard horror stories about the friction close friends experienced in working together for extended periods of time, but Carrie's and my friendship had gone from strength to strength – no mean feat when you considered all the changes we'd been through since we first met. We were relatively energetic 22- and 24-year-olds when we started out (Carrie's younger, as she loves to remind me), and now here we were, a married mother of two and me, a soon-to-be-bride. Carrie had married her long-term partner, John, a few years into her teaching career, and they were basically picture-perfect models of monogamy and contentedness. Together with their adorable children, Lachlan and my Goddaughter Aria, they could have been a family from a sitcom. Back in the early days of my relationship with Adam I used to love spending time at their house and cuddling a then-infant Aria, hoping my life would turn out as perfectly as Carrie's seemed to have. It should have been nauseating, but somehow, it wasn't.

"Anyway," Georgia continued, "I was just coming to check if you guys were up for an iced chockie break."

The three of us could all afford to retire if we had a dollar for every time one of us suggested an iced chockie break. It was a warm day, so Carrie and I quickly agreed. "I can't stay for too long, though," Carrie added. "It's my day to pick the kids up."

"That's fine, I don't want to be too late either. Adam's cooking dinner tonight," I said. "I have to arrive home with an appetite." My friends immediately leapt on my poor choice of words, engaging in an over-exaggerated show of winking and nudging each other. I rolled my eyes and grinned but the truth was, I was hoping tonight wouldn't stop at just dinner. It had been a while. I thought dry spells weren't supposed to happen until after the wedding, I mused as we grabbed our bags and closed up Carrie's classroom.

"We'll have to stop our iced chocolates soon, of course," Carrie said, "if we're to fit in our dresses and all!" The two girls were going to be bridesmaids on my big day, along with my younger sister Julie, and we had all vowed to help each other get into shape. It hadn't worked so far. Julie was the only one who had actually started watching her food intake, and she was the one who didn't have any weight to lose. I should probably care more about my lack of willpower than I did, but I was pretty happy to walk down the aisle the way I was.

"Yeah. That'll happen," Georgia said, deadpan, summing up my thoughts as well. The three of us piled into my car – by unspoken agreement I always seemed to be the chauffer of the group, even though my driving could generously be described as erratic. The tiny, family-run café we frequented was only a few minutes down the road, but at the end of a long day the last thing we felt like doing was walking. As I drove the three of us sang along to the radio at top note, not caring whether we were off-key. When we got there, I ordered a cinnamon doughnut as well as my drink, and the girls, taking their cue from me, did the same. We could usually be counted on to be mutually bad influences on each other.

I talked about wanting to lose weight for my wedding, but the truth was I'd never been one of those women who had grand plans for her wedding day. The wedding didn't really concern me; I just wanted to be married. I had met Adam when I was 30, after years of being unlucky in love, and we got engaged three years later. Now 34, I was eager to get the wedding plans over and done with so I could begin married life.

Adam and I had met online, as everyone seemed to nowadays. I was instantly attracted to the image of his warm, friendly eyes and his dimples, but the conversation over email hadn't really lit my fire the way I'd hoped, and I nearly hadn't met up with him at all. It was Georgia who convinced me to go, pointing out that the worst-case scenario was that I'd have additional dating practice for when the right guy did come along. "Actually, the worst-case scenario is that he rapes me behind a dumpster," I'd replied tartly, but I'd given in and gone along, and over gnocchi and a side salad, I'd felt a connection. I'd always thought the best part of dating was grabbing breakfast with the girls the following morning and dissecting the night, but when it came to Adam, it felt more like something I wanted to keep to myself. I didn't want to participate in our usual ranking system – scores out of a possible ten for his looks, his behaviour, the conversation, the chemistry – and that, more than anything, was how I knew that Adam was something special.

I had long ago resigned myself to the idea of a solo life, having been single for the great majority of my twenties. I had nearly given up on marriage and motherhood entirely, an idea that now seemed completely foreign to me. I had always wanted to be a mother, and I could barely wait until the wedding night to start trying. When Adam had appeared, he had completely swept me off my feet, long after I thought that kind of thing was behind me. The spark had dulled a bit since then, but that was just human nature. No relationship remained the same from the beginning through to marriage. Life wasn't a romantic comedy, after all. The reality sometimes seemed to fall a bit short, but that wasn't to say it wasn't enough.

# Chapter 2

That night I let myself into my home and felt my shoulders instantly relax. My class was on the challenging side this year and iced chocolate dates with the girls were great, but home was my safe haven at the end of a hard day. Adam was in the kitchen, cooking a stir-fry, and I went up and wrapped my hands around him from behind. "Hey, babe," I murmured. "How was your day?"

"Oh, the usual," Adam replied, turning and kissing me lightly on the forehead. He was a banker, and his responses about his work were usually ambivalent. I felt lucky to have a job I was truly passionate about, even though some days felt like they lasted an eternity. "How was yours?"

I let go of my fiancé and went and perched on one of our retro-style red bar stools as I filled him in on the highlights of my day – the kid who couldn't read a word at the start of the year and now had a bank of sight words; the boy with the great sense of humour making another perfectly timed pun; the Year Six teacher who was trying to organise a staff versus students basketball game for the following afternoon. I didn't mention my afternoon with the girls, though. It was easier to just let Adam assume I was marking work or preparing things for tomorrow rather than having fun while he worked and then came home to cook.

There were studies done on how many words women speak in a day compared with men, but I often felt like the researchers could have saved some effort and just observed Adam and me for a day. He was introspective, always leaving the lion's share of conversation up to me. On the plus side, he was a reasonably good listener and I was more than happy to speak for two, so it worked for us.

"Sounds great. Why don't you pour us some wine? Dinner's nearly ready." He sounded slightly distracted, but I put it down to something that happened at work. Something I wouldn't hear about unless he deemed it necessary to tell me.

I grabbed a red and poured up to the line marked on the glasses we'd gotten for our engagement. I knew we'd finish the bottle between us that night. I was never much of a wine drinker before I met Adam, especially not red wine, but he'd helped me develop a taste for it. Perhaps unusually for a guy his age, wine had always been Adam's drink of choice over beer. I personally was partial to vodka and cocktails, but wine seemed like such a social choice that I was pleased to have developed a liking for it. I never could bring myself to drink coffee, so red wine felt like my one concession towards a 'grown up' drink.

"I thought we might have Jack over this weekend," I said as I carried the glasses over to the couch. "It's been a while since you guys have seen each other." Jack and I usually caught up once a week, but the two men saw a lot less of each other. Adam hadn't known Jack was gay when I first started telling him stories about my good friend, and although he now obviously realised that Jack posed no threat, he'd never quite come around to him the way I had hoped. Part of me thought that Adam felt like he had to share me with another man, although he'd never come out and said that. It was ridiculous, but human nature often defied logic. I didn't agree with Adam's point of view, but I tried to respect it.

Adam grimaced as he brought the bowls of stir-fry over and sat beside me on the couch. "Can't we just have a quiet one this weekend?"

"Adam," I sighed, "we've had a quiet one *every* weekend lately. I feel like we're an old married couple already, and we haven't even got to the wedding day yet!" I tried, somewhat unsuccessfully, to keep my tone light. This was the sort of conversation we were having all the time lately, and it usually led to the same thing – us going along with what he wanted, sitting on the couch alone. I wasn't willing to give in quite so easily this time. "It'll be fun. You can invite Derek and Belinda around, too, if you want?" Derek was Adam's oldest friend, who was going to be Best Man at our wedding. He and Jack had only met a couple of times, but Jack made conversation easily with anyone, and Derek's wife was a sweetheart.

Adam shook his head and stared down at his food. He was silent for several minutes, while I frowned over at him. He was quieter than I expected tonight, even from him. Something was clearly wrong. I was about to ask what it was when he spoke again.

"I can't do this," he muttered, his voice hoarse.

I rolled my eyes. "*Fine,* we'll have a quiet weekend, but you do know I want to have dinner parties more regularly after the wedding. We can't just sit at home and stare at the walls all the time!" I loved a quiet night in, but I was also always up for socialising. All I wanted was a bit of balance.

"No. I can't do this," Adam repeated. His voice was an odd monotone, as if he were discussing something completely innocuous. "Us. I can't do it anymore."

"Um, I'm sorry? What do you mean?" My heart seemed to catch in my throat. I tried to tell myself I had misunderstood him, even though a larger part of me knew I hadn't. I couldn't fathom how we'd gone from a casual discussion to a break-up so quickly.

"I'm sorry, Annie. I've been thinking it for a while. I wasn't going to do this tonight, but there's no right time. I loved you, but I just can't marry you. I never should have asked."

My heart stopped. "You're joking, right?" I asked stupidly, as if he would joke about something like that. One minute we were talking about dinner parties, and the next he was leaving me? My mind slowly registered on his past tense. He *loved* me. "What the fuck, Adam? Is there someone else?"

"No," he answered after a beat, but the way he moved his eyes sideways, away from my face, told me everything I needed to know.

"Screw you, Adam," I said through the lump in my throat. "Who is she?"

He at least had the decency to look uncomfortable. "That's not important, Annie," he mumbled. "It's just not going to work, okay?"

"You're disgusting," I spat out, tears running freely down my face now, made up of equal parts sadness and anger. It was as if I could actually feel my heart breaking in my chest. "Wasn't I enough for you? I would have had sex more often, you know."

I paused and looked at him through my tears, pleadingly. "I would have tried more things." Deep down, I knew that wasn't the problem. If anything, I'd had the higher libido than Adam lately, which probably should have been a sign.

"It's not about that," Adam said, shaking his head miserably. "It's just not right, Annie. We're not right. Trust me, it's better that I'm ending it now than after years of marriage... after *kids*. Just walk away. It doesn't have to be complicated." He shrugged. He actually shrugged. I had never hated anyone more than I did right then and there, with that stupid bloody shrug.

"It doesn't have to be *complicated*, you asshole!" I screamed, surprising even myself with the rage in my voice. "Of course it's *complicated!* We're engaged. *I love you*!" I stared at him, and I noticed how aside from an almost imperceptible flinch, his face didn't even change when I said those three words. "But I guess that doesn't matter," I added in a smaller voice. "I thought you loved me, too, but obviously you love... *her.* Whoever she is."

"Annie, don't," Adam said, his voice softer now.

"Whatever," I said, suddenly more resigned than angry. "I can't make you love me, I can't make you stay with me, so now I guess you get to go off and be happy with your mystery woman, and I can go off and be single and miserable and just try to forget you ever existed." I stood up and went to the door, not really knowing where I was planning to go, but knowing I needed to get the hell out of there. I grabbed my handbag, which I'd thrown so casually onto the dining table chair when I'd walked in, expecting it to be just another Thursday night. "I'll text you so I know when you're going to be out and I can come to get my things. I hope you have a wonderful life. I really don't ever want to see you again." And just like that, without even a change of clothes, I walked out of the life I thought I was going to lead.

# Chapter 3

Thankfully I hadn't made it through more than two sips of my wine, so I was at least able to drive myself away from Adam. There was nothing less dignified than storming out and then having to stand by the side of the road awaiting a lift. I got down the street before pulling over to think about where I could go. I wasn't ready to face my family that night – I needed to clear my head before I was ready to tell them about the broken engagement – and I knew Jack was working late. I didn't really want to see Carrie's happy family right now, either. I called Georgia, who answered on the second ring. "Hey!" she exclaimed cheerfully. Of course she couldn't have known why I was calling, but I still somehow expected her to sound as bleak as I felt, and her enthusiastic voice provided a stark contrast to my state of mind. "Annie?" she prompted when I didn't say anything.

I found my voice. "Can I stay the night?"

I could hear the concern in Georgia's voice as she asked if I was okay. "I'm fine," I lied. "I just need a place to stay. Be there in 15? Oh, and Georgia? I don't have a change of clothes or anything."

"I'll put out some PJs," she said immediately. "I should have something for you to wear tomorrow, too."

"PJs will do," I said, switching the phone to Bluetooth and beginning to drive towards my friend's house. "I don't think I'll be going anywhere for a while."

AFTER THAT CONVERSATION, my tear-streaked appearance didn't come as much of a surprise to Georgia when she opened the door to me and grabbed me immediately into an embrace. "Oh, Annie, are you okay?" she whispered, stroking my hair. "What happened? Did you guys have a fight?"

"More than a fight," I said, letting out a bark of a laugh that was completely devoid of humour. "Adam's called the wedding off. There's someone else." The words felt so unreal. An hour earlier, I'd been engaged. I looked down at my hand. I was still wearing my ring.

Georgia's mouth dropped open ever so slightly. "I – oh my God, I don't know what to say. I'm so sorry, Annie!" she cried, hugging me again, tighter this time. "Come in, come in. Do your parents know?" Georgia was what Carrie and I described as 'abnormally' close with her own parents, and I knew they would have been the first people she told in this situation. Carrie and I often joked about their relationship, but deep down I envied it.

I shook my head. "You're the first person I've told. It feels so weird, saying it out loud." I walked into her house and looked around. Georgia's house was always on the messy side, but in a comforting, lived-in way. "Is Michael here?"

"No, he's with his dad tonight. It's just us girls."

Georgia had become pregnant at 20, long before I met her. Surprisingly, her fledgling relationship had survived the unexpected birth of their son Michael, and Georgia and Scott had married six years later. Perhaps less surprisingly, Scott had left her last year, one month before Georgia's mum was diagnosed with cancer. The timing made me hate him a little bit more than I would have anyway, despite knowing that Scott couldn't have possibly predicted what was to come. The upshot of both the cancer and the separation was that Georgia's relationship with her parents had become even closer than it already was, and she had toyed with the idea of moving herself and Michael into their spacious family home before realising she wanted to make up for "lost time", which basically meant having plenty of no-strings-attached sex. Michael was 14 now so she had to be careful about bringing men home, but she and Scott had split custody and so far, Georgia had made amends for her lost time rather admirably. I couldn't deny that Carrie and I loved hearing her stories, living vicariously through her, since we were both in supposedly stable relationships that sometimes lacked spontaneity. I definitely hadn't envied her, though, and now here I was, in the same boat. I didn't think I could embrace the single life as easily as Georgia had done.

"Are you ready to talk about it?" Georgia asked as I went and sat on the couch. "I have vodka, but no ice cream, I'm sorry to say."

I suddenly realised how hungry I was – I hadn't actually touched any of the amazing-smelling stir-fry Adam had made before I stormed out. The prick could have at least let me eat before dropping his bombshell. "I haven't eaten," I admitted. "Have you?"

"Not yet." It felt like midnight, but it was actually just after 7, and Georgia famously admitted to not putting in much effort food-wise on the nights her son wasn't with her. "I was just going to have a frozen meal, but I'm guessing your blues call for a bit more than that?"

I grimaced. "Definitely," I replied, not wanting to sound ungrateful, but feeling like I needed a more substantial meal.

"Not a problem. Pizza? Indian? You order whatever you like and I'll call Ann-Marie about tomorrow. You're not going to work in this state, and I'm not going to leave you either. And don't even think about doing a relief plan! One day without a plan won't hurt anybody." Her voice was firm, more like the one I'd heard her use with Michael or her students than any tone she'd ever taken with me.

"What are you going to tell her?" The idea of my Principal knowing she was two staff members down for the day because my fiancé had left me didn't exactly excite me.

"I'll just say you're having a family situation and I'm working through it with you. Or group food poisoning? Carrie could catch it too?"

I smiled in spite of myself. "The first one's okay. They'll all find out about it when I don't get married in six months, anyway! Make your call and I'll get some Indian, and then I'll call Caz."

CARRIE WAS SHOCKED and sympathetic and immediately offered to take the following day off as well so she could come over, but I told her not to. I knew she was low on sick leave after having time off whenever one of her kids was sick, and besides, the three of us all taking the day off might push Ann-Marie over the edge, especially considering how suspicious it would look on a Friday! John obviously picked up on the fact that something was wrong from Carrie's end of the conversation, and I could hear his voice in the background urging her to come over straight away. John could always be relied on to look after the kids for the sake of a girls' night, especially at a time like this.

"Just a sec," Carrie said, and she must have moved the phone away as she murmured to her husband in the background. Her voice came back on the line. "John's going to look after the kids and I'm coming over. I'll be there in 20." I looked at Georgia, who was listening on loudspeaker, and she gave me a thumbs up sign.

"We've already ordered dinner," I said guiltily. I should have predicted that Carrie would drop everything and come to be with me.

"It's fine, we already ate. Do you want me to bring anything?"

I looked at Georgia. "Ice cream," we said in one voice.

# Chapter 4

Georgia and Carrie sat on the couch together while I sat on the floor cushion in front, still numb with shock. How was it possible that three hours earlier I'd been engaged and now I was cross-legged on my friend's floor, soothing my pain with fatty food and vodka? We sat mostly in silence, the other two not knowing what to say and me not yet ready to put my feelings into words. Finally, I spoke.

"He has another woman," I said, as if that was new information rather than something I'd already told them both. "I just don't get that. Where did he meet her? He doesn't even bloody go anywhere. He barely had enough energy for one partner, so I don't know how he managed two of us." I paused for breath, but only briefly. "How long has it been going on? Why is she so amazing he wants to leave the woman he was *engaged* to for her? How could I not have seen this coming? And what's her name?" I finished, my voice breaking at the end of my tirade. I sniffled and took another sip of my vodka and lime.

"He's an asshat," Carrie said firmly, using her favourite word for anyone who gave her grief. "He'll live to regret this, you'll see. You're amazing, and any guy would be lucky to have you, and now he's with someone who'll probably cheat on him in return in a few weeks."

"He said we weren't right together," I spat out, as if my friend hadn't spoken. "It's not like he was Mr Perfect, you know. I had my issues with him too, but I didn't just *quit*! We were going to get married! You can't just quit on someone because something newer and shinier comes along." I paused. "But what if he *doesn't* live to regret it? What if they get married and live happily ever after and I'm stuck here with no one?" The tears started flowing again.

"It's not going to happen," replied Georgia at the same time Carrie said "you'll never be alone". I wasn't sure of Georgia's statement, but I knew Carrie was right. I had plenty of people in my corner, and I knew I could count on their support.

"I'm so lucky to have you guys," I said mournfully, looking up at my best friends. "Seriously, I don't know what I'd do without you."

"Uh-oh," Georgia said, laughing to lighten the moment. "She's at *that* stage of drunk." She slurred her words in an exaggerated impression of me. "'I love you all so much!'"

I smiled at her efforts to cheer me up. Carrie was always there to give sage advice in a crisis, while Georgia could be counted on to provide lame jokes to make me smile. "That's me, Drunky McDrunk," I said lightly.

"So what's happening with your place?" Carrie asked, a serious look coming into your eyes. "Who's going to move out?"

I shrugged. "We were only renting after all, so that part should be pretty easy. It was Adam's place first, so he can stay there as far as I'm concerned. He can move Bimbo McGee in with him if he really wants to! It has too many bad memories. Too many memories, full stop."

"And what about you?" Carrie asked. "Will you find a place of your own?"

I closed my eyes. "I'm not ready to think about that just yet," I responded faintly. "It's a little too much reality for tonight."

My friends nodded reassuringly, and Georgia cleared her throat. "Speaking of reality, I've got the last two episodes of *Top Model* on my hard drive. Shall we?"

SEVERAL HOURS OF MIND-numbing television later, Carrie said her goodbyes, hugging me a little closer and a little longer than usual. "You'll be fine," she whispered in my ear before she left. "We're all here for you." I smiled thinly and patted her back. I suppose deep down I knew I would make it through, but I couldn't see the way just yet.

Georgia, ever the welcoming hostess, went upstairs and made my bed up for me. When I entered the spare room, I found chocolates on my pillow and a stack of books and magazines on the bedside table for me to choose from. I was relieved to find the books were mostly thrillers or crime fiction, nothing in the least bit romantic. "Some of my favourites," she said, nodding at the reading materials, "and some trashy mags thrown in for good measure. I figured they might help a bit. I've got a new toothbrush in the bathroom for you, and I can lend you some moisturiser and whatever you need. I'm sure we can find a time this weekend to go pick up your things, but you're welcome to stay as long as you need."

"Thank you," I said, humbled by her generosity. I was so lucky to have such good friends.

We said our farewells and I crawled into bed. I was sure I wouldn't sleep at all, but after reading a few pages I discovered I couldn't keep my eyes open, and the next thing I knew it was morning.

# Chapter 5

"Good morning, sunshine!" Georgia cried out when I entered the kitchen. I was still in my borrowed pyjamas, but Georgia looked like she'd been up for hours. She was wearing a casual maxi-dress with her hair up in a tight ponytail and she was throwing fruit into her blender to make smoothies, like a good 1950s housewife. I sat down at her kitchen table. "God, you're such a *Mum,*" I said, but not without affection. "How long have you been up?" I glanced down at my phone and saw to my surprise that it was already nine o'clock.

"Just an hour," Georgia said dismissively. "That spa we went to last holidays isn't open yet, but I thought we could try to book in for massages, and then maybe go to lunch. Or just for dessert."

"That sounds amazing," I replied honestly, "but maybe tomorrow would be better. I think I need to stay in my pyjamas today... well, your pyjamas... and watch some DVDs. Is that okay?"

"Of course! Your wish is my command," Georgia said, pushing my smoothie across the table to me.

The rest of the day was spent mostly on Georgia's couch, watching action movies and eating leftover butter chicken. In the afternoon I knew I couldn't put it off anymore and called

Mum to tell her the news. She was empathetic and tried to act strong, but I could hear her starting to sniffle a bit towards the end of our conversation and I felt terrible for upsetting her. One of my least favourite things about getting older was how we started to worry about our parents, when it had always been the other way around.

Mum promised to let Julie know, which was a relief – one less call I'd have to make. Dad took the phone and offered some gruff yet supportive words. My Dad was a man of few words, preferring to take things in than to talk a lot, but I knew he'd do anything for me. He offered their place for me to stay at, but I told him I was staying with Georgia for the short term and that I'd let him know when I needed some help with the moving process. Of course, I could go and take things from my house as much as I wanted, but where the hell was I going to put them?

I CALLED JACK STRAIGHT after Mum and Dad to tell him the news, and he immediately asked if he could come to Georgia's after work to see me. Georgia had always liked Jack, although they hadn't had a lot to do with each other. She said that he was welcome, of course, on the proviso that he came bearing wine. I've never been as grateful to see anyone as when I opened the door to Jack, who was holding flowers as well as the promised bottle of Moscato.

"Babe!" he said, grabbing me in a big hug, and suddenly I was transported back to when I'd first met Jack, when I would have given anything for him to turn up with flowers for me.

# Chapter 6

I had fallen in love with Jack pretty quickly after I met him. Even in previous relationships, I'd never before felt the chemistry I shared with Jack. Looking back now, knowing he was gay, it was hard to remember the depths of my feelings, but at the time they'd been completely real for me. I had the sort of crush that was only really socially acceptable coming from a teenager, not a grown woman in her twenties. I was besotted. Every sappy love song I heard made me think of him. I used to daydream about the day when we would get together, about our wedding day. I was about five minutes away from doodling "Mrs Annabel Delaney" on my notebook in little hearts. It was embarrassing to think back about, but I honestly couldn't blame myself for falling so hard. I had never met anyone before who seemed to get me the way he did, and it was irresistible. His good looks and kind nature didn't hurt, either.

It was with startling clarity that I could recall the day Jack invited me out to breakfast on a Saturday morning, nearly ten years earlier, about four months into our friendship. We went to a casual, open-air café with a cheery, Bohemian feel. I propped a purple cushion behind my back as I sat on the wicker chair and opened my menu, thinking of nothing more than what I wanted to eat. It was 9:30 already, and I was starving.

It sounds dramatic but when I looked back, I would always remember that cheerful purple cushion.

As I was casually deciding between honeycomb pancakes and eggs benedict, I glanced at Jack and realised how nervous he was. "Are you okay?" I asked, surprised. I knew him well enough by now to realise he wasn't himself.

Just then the waiter turned up, interrupting us before Jack could reply. We placed our order (I opted for the pancakes) and I looked back at Jack, raising an eyebrow. I tried to keep calm, but his demeanour was making me nervous as well. Was this it? Was he finally going to admit to having feelings for me? I'd considered telling him about my own feelings, but kept getting nervous. Our friendship was amazing and I didn't want to ruin anything, but I also knew I couldn't go on much longer as platonic friends when I wanted us to be so much more. Now, just maybe, he was going to beat me to it.

"Annie, you're such an amazing friend to me," Jack blurted out, as if he couldn't get his words out quickly enough to match his thoughts. "I know I should have told you sooner, but it's never easy." I closed my eyes in anticipation of his words. *Yes, this is it!* "Annie," Jack said, his voice cracking a little, "I... I'm gay."

The world stopped spinning, just for a minute. I kept my eyes closed, squeezing them tighter, hoping that when I woke up I would find myself in bed, that it would all be a dream. Jack kept speaking. "My family knows, and the friends I've had for ages, but I'm a pretty private person and I just don't like to let people know too much, too soon. I'm single at the moment, but I still feel like I have to tell you the truth."

I nodded slowly, letting out a deep, shaky breath. When I opened my eyes, they were filled with tears which I desperately tried to will away. I didn't want Jack to think I was upset with him in any way. When I spoke, my voice didn't sound like my own. "Jack, I'm so glad you told me," I said slowly, finally meeting his eyes, those amazing deep blue eyes. "I have to say I'm surprised... I never would have picked it. But we're friends, and nothing is going to change that."

A huge, relieved smile broke out on Jack's face. "Annie, you're the best," he said softly, but all I could think, however illogically, was *but not good enough*.

Later Jack would confess to me that he knew about the feelings I had developed for him, and he had decided to tell me before I was any further invested. To be honest, that was one confession I could have lived without. Even as time passed and I started to truly see him as nothing more than a friend, or even as a brother, I worried that he would think I hugged him too tightly, or that I smiled too widely when I greeted him; that I was still trying to hide deeper feelings for him. There was nothing to do about it, though, except to stop seeing him altogether, and that was something I couldn't manage. If I could only have his friendship... well, that was more than enough.

"I DON'T KNOW WHAT TO do," I said now, literally crying on Jack's shoulder. "I can't afford to live alone, and I don't know how, anyway. I lived with my family, then a roommate, then Adam. I'm pathetic. I'm going to have to move back in with my parents at 34. I'm a trainwreck!"

"Oh my God, you can be so dramatic," Jack said, his voice more light-hearted than his words. "You don't have to move in with mumsy and daddy again, and you won't be living on the street, either. Come move in with me! I have that spare room just sitting there doing nothing."

"You *like* having a spare room," I reminded him, sniffling. Jack had often proclaimed he had "no houseguests – at least none who need a bed of their own", and therefore turned the spare room into his games room, complete with a full-sized air hockey table and a collection of retro-themed pinball machines displayed proudly and prominently around the room.

"I don't! Well, I do. But I like you more." Jack nudged me. "Plus, if I live with you I won't have to talk to myself so often. Come on, it'll be fun. Do it!"

It all happened fairly quickly after that. Jack moved his air hockey table into the garage and the pinball machines into his own room, then my moving van and I turned up the following weekend. Georgia had been an amazing host, but I knew she was happy to get life back to normal. Michael had been home the last few nights, and although he was a sweet kid, I wasn't quite ready for life with a teenaged boy. My parents and Julie all came along to help with the moving process, and before long Jack's spare room looked like it had belonged to me all along.

My parents cautioned me that I shouldn't get myself locked into paying rent forever, but the price Jack was charging me was pretty fair and I'd never had any grand ambitions of owning my own home; at least, not until I had someone to share the mortgage with. Moving in with Jack felt like creating some kind of modern Dream Home all our own.

The house itself was gorgeous – light and airy, with a huge living room in which we could picture ourselves hosting amazing parties. Jack had never really been much of an entertainer before, but we laughed about the idea of a 'woman's touch' being the missing element. In other words, he meant he was too lazy! The house was, of course, fully furnished already and some of my things from my life with Adam had to go into storage, but my smaller items were able to come with me. I put my own touch on the place as much as I thought I could get away with, considering Jack was the one paying the mortgage. For two extremely similar people, our taste when it came to home decorating couldn't have been more different. He loved monochrome colours and a simple aesthetic, whereas I was a sucker for any bright colours and patterns I could find. I'd always privately thought his cream leather couch was a little plain next to the cream walls of the house, so I threw in some brightly coloured blue and yellow cushions to spruce it up a bit. Jack loved adorning the house with candles – one of the few signs that the guy living there was gay, I supposed – and I did my part by buying fresh, brightly-coloured flowers every week, displaying most of them in my large vase on the table and trimming some down to put in an old lemonade bottle that I'd repurposed. The place was starting to look and feel like home. This was what I loved about my friendship with Jack: everything always felt so *easy* with him, so comfortable.

Jack's mum Heather was a quilter from long ago, so she made us each a quilt in honour of my arrival – a manly-looking creation of deep greens and browns for Jack, and a gorgeous patchwork of bright colours for me. "It's funny," I said to Jack when we took our new quilts home. "You wouldn't think it, but the contrast sort of sets it off and they go together kind of perfectly."

Jack grinned at me. "I would think it, actually," he said.

LIVING WITH JACK WAS everything I had hoped, and to be honest, a hell of a lot easier than living with Adam had ever been. We took turns cooking and divided the cleaning evenly. We still had our own lives, of course, but every Monday we put aside as "Date Night". We would order takeaway and either snuggle under our quilts and watch a DVD, or play board games, or go out bowling, or whatever took our fancy. I'd always used music to wake myself up in the morning, so we would blast our current musical obsession through our iPod speakers in the morning and find ourselves dancing around the house as we got ready for work. He would almost always beat me out the door, not because I was spending so long getting ready, but because I would get distracted by one small thing or another. He'd be eating breakfast while I was still idly checking Facebook or wondering about making a cup of tea.

Jack was also always open to the idea of me having people over, so I entertained more in my first month there than I had in the past year with Adam. It was usually just Carrie and Georgia coming to visit, or sometimes my sister Julie, but it was nice to feel like I could invite people over at the drop of a hat rather than having to work around someone else's schedule. It was crazy that I should feel more at home here than I had living with my own fiancé. God, why hadn't I realised how bad things had been with Adam?

Most nights Jack would open a bottle of wine and talk about our working day. Honestly, if you compared us to a normal, happy relationship it was hard to think of much we were missing. Okay, sex, obviously, but I was reasonably happy to take matters into my own hands, so to speak. It wasn't like that element of my relationship with Adam was ever worth writing home about anyway. I wasn't ready to date yet, but Jack went on dates semi-regularly, although he never seemed to find anyone too serious. To be honest, I was secretly glad of that. I didn't know how a significant partner – for either of us – would fit into what we had.

# Chapter 7

As my latest "screw you" to Adam, I decided to start going to the gym more regularly. I took some amount of feminist pride in acknowledging that this decision had little to do with him and more to do with looking and feeling good for myself post-breakup. My sister had tried to persuade me to join her gym for a while, and I'd finally relented six months earlier. To my surprise, I actually did enjoy it – when I managed to make it there. I struggled to get there once or twice a week while Julie went in every day like clockwork, befriending the staff and fellow exercisers and generally running around like she owned the place.

For two people raised in the same household by the same parents, my sister and I couldn't have been more different. I was laidback, cared more about comfort than style, and my idea of a good time was being curled up in my room with a good book. At five years younger than me, Julie was a self-confessed 'princess' and a party girl who never planned to settle down. She was happily childfree, and said she wouldn't have kids even if she met Mr Right tomorrow. Part of me envied her for that. It had to be easier than pining for something you couldn't have. Julie just seemed completely happy with her life in a way I wasn't sure I had ever been.

Her devotion to the gym, as well as her vegan diet, had resulted in a slim figure and amazing calf muscles. I was pretty envious of her smaller frame, but not to the extent of doing much about it. The gym was the only place you'd catch her bare-faced – even a trip to the grocery store warranted a full face of make-up, whereas I was lucky to put on a bra to duck down to the shops. We weren't as close as I'd have liked, although we were getting closer as we got older. Nevertheless, I would still go to Carrie, Georgia or Jack over seeking my sister out for advice.

It was no surprise to see Julie's car parked at the gym when I pulled up on a Monday afternoon. It was about two months since the break-up – two months post-Adam, as I'd started to refer to it. It was my third visit in a week, which was almost a record for me. More surprising was the sudden and disturbing realisation that my joggers were nowhere to be seen. I searched through my car frantically, knowing that if they weren't here, there was no way I was going home for them and coming back again. Julie always told me not to drive barefoot, but it was a habit from a long time ago. Where the hell had they gone? I groaned, suddenly remembering walking into the house with them after my last trip two days earlier, in an unusual attempt to keep my car tidy. It was further proof that cleaning was never worth it. Eventually I found a pair of flat loafer-style shoes: neither the most supportive nor the best looking with my green socks (which already weren't the best combination with my blue tights), but they'd have to do.

I added the last piece to my awkward ensemble and walked through the gym into the locker room, trying not to feel self-conscious. Who cared what you wore to the *gym*, anyway?

"AND THAT'S WHEN I RAN into my sister," I said, my tone deliberately solemn, as I filled Jack in on my day.

"Oh, grim," he said, topping up my glass. "So I'm guessing darling Julie had something to say about your ensemble?" He pronounced *ensemble* with an exaggerated French accent.

"Yep," I sighed. "I was actually on the exercise bike and I saw her walk past and didn't call out to her because I didn't want the clothing lecture. She sailed right past me and I thought I was safe, but then... she saw my car and glanced back in. Of course, it was the *one* damn day where I got a park right near the door." I took a sip of my lemonade, more to create a pause for effect than out of thirst. "It was like something out of a horror movie – you think you're safe, the serial killer walks past and doesn't see your hiding spot, and then *bam*." I slammed the heel of my hand down on the table for emphasis. "The killer spots you, turns in slow motion towards you..."

"And insults your shoes," Jack finished, laughing. I loved to hear people laugh when I told them my stories, which were always complete with large and unwieldy hand flourishes. Truth be told, part of me, even when something was happening, was already drafting the story in my head as to how I was going to share it with my friends. I couldn't figure out if that was a bad thing – I should Live in the Moment! – or a good thing – I had friends with whom I wanted to share my life! Maybe it was a bit of both.

It was date night, and Jack and I had decided this week's theme was drinking and chatting. It was a more simple theme than usual, but it worked. It had been a busy week for both of us, and we hadn't caught up properly in a while. Having some downtime to chat together was just what we needed.

"So that was my day," I finished off. "How was yours?"

Jack rolled his eyes. He worked in promotions for a local radio station, and his work stories were always interesting. He filled me in on the argument he'd had that morning with a particularly demanding customer and soon had me laughing.

"On a serious note, though," Jack said when we'd finished our chat about our day, "how are you coping with everything?"

I sighed, knowing he meant life post-Adam. "It's weird," I admitted. "I actually don't feel as bad as I feel like I should, if that makes sense? I mean, obviously it's not the ideal situation, and telling everyone the wedding's off sucked, but I feel like I'm missing the idea of him more than the actual guy. I don't want to see him again. If he came around tomorrow begging to have me back, I'd tell him where to go. But... it's still a shitty situation, obviously. I should be a few months away from my wedding right now and instead I'm bitching about my love life with you." I paused. "Not that I'm not entirely grateful about our living situation, of course."

"Please. I'm just a bed to you." Jack paused, as if trying to figure out how to ask something delicate. "Do you think you're sad about not being married to him, or about not having your wedding day?"

"Oh, it's definitely not the wedding day," I replied immediately. "You know I never cared much about that. I think Georgia's more upset to have lost out on a bridesmaid gig." I laughed lightly and then paused. "It's not really the fact of not being married to Adam, either," I added slowly. "I think it's more the idea of not being married... in general. I mean, I'm nearly 35 and I'm single. Even if I meet the right person tomorrow, marriage and babies are still years away. It's hard, that's all."

Jack put a sympathetic hand on my shoulder. "Hey, I get it. I never thought babies were on the cards for me. Now same-sex couples are getting married and having babies left and right, but I don't exactly have men lining up at my door waiting to raise babies with me. I guess I just thought life would be further along by now."

I nodded silently, taking his words in. That summed up my feelings on the topic fairly well. I hadn't been able to put it into words yet, hadn't even tried, but it felt like life was a race to the finish line and I was stumbling around far behind everyone else, still on my own while my friends' children were growing up around me. As close as I was to Georgia and Carrie, sometimes it felt like they were part of some exclusive club that I could just watch from the outside.

Every so often, usually at the end of the year, people would go crazy with "ten year challenge!" photos and updates on social media, and I couldn't help but feel a twinge when I saw the posts. Most of my friends were sharing images of their weddings and the babies born in the past ten years. Where had a decade taken me? It struck me, not for the first time, that without weddings and babies, I didn't have much to show for my time. Realistically, I knew that wasn't true. All I had to do was think of the children I'd taught over the last ten years. If I had a lasting impact on even one or two from each class, that couldn't be overlooked. Besides which, I had great friends surrounding me and a fairly active social life. Plenty of people never had babies and lived rich, fulfilling lives. And yet, mine didn't feel complete.

I loved Carrie and Georgia's kids like they were my own nieces and nephews, but simply being surrounded by children wasn't the same as having one of your own. I had always expected to be a mum someday, and the idea of that not coming true was almost too much to bear. Unexpectedly, tears started slipping down my cheeks.

"Oh, Annie, I'm sorry! I didn't mean to upset you." Jack was slightly better with tears than a lot of guys our age, but only slightly. His discomfort was clear. "We can talk about something else. Tell me what Lewis got up to today," he added, naming one of my livelier class members.

I shook my head. "It's okay, we don't have to change the subject. I just haven't really let myself think about the whole kid thing much since Adam left. I don't miss him," I added, honestly. "I know it wasn't right. But sometimes I feel like even being in the wrong marriage would be worth it so I could have a family of my own." I hated hearing the words come out of my own mouth. They made me sound so pathetic. What sort of a doormat sat there and willingly admitted she'd happily settle, if the guy she'd planned to settle with was willing to let her? It surprised even me to hear my own thoughts.

We were quiet for a few minutes, and then Jack asked, "would you ever go it alone?"

"Having a baby, you mean? I don't know. I've never really had to think about it," I said. "Having babies was kind of an abstract thing in my twenties. Then I met Adam and just assumed I'd be having my kids with him. This is the first time I've had to imagine a future without kids, and it sucks! So yeah, I guess I'd consider it, but I'd have to have my life a lot more in order.

I mean, I can't pop out a baby while I'm living in your spare room." I laughed at the absurdity of it all.

Jack didn't laugh with me. He stared at me for a long time, as if wrestling with whether to say what he was thinking. When he finally opened his mouth, the words that came out were, somehow, simultaneously surprising and expected. "Why not?"

# Chapter 8

I stared at Jack, trying to figure out how to put into words what I wanted to say. I finally managed to get out a question. "What do you mean?"

Jack shrugged and looked down for a minute, suddenly seeming a lot younger than his 35 years. "It's probably a crazy idea, but you want a baby, I want a baby. I'm single, you're single. We get along better than most couples! Would it be the strangest thing in the world if we did it together?"

My mouth, or possibly my brain, seemed to stop working. I'd never been speechless before, but this stopped me in my tracks. I turned Jack's question over in my head, trying to think of a reason as to exactly why his proposal wouldn't work, but I came up empty. Obviously it wasn't the situation I'd always dreamt of when I'd pictured creating a family, but having my fiancé walk out on me for another woman wasn't exactly a dream scenario, either. Being single at 34 was never part of my plan. What was the alternative? Wait and try to meet someone new? Even if this elusive mystery man did come along, there was no guarantee that I would be able to have babies with him by the time our relationship finally progressed to that stage. There was no guarantee we wouldn't have kids and then break up. Doing it with Jack would mean going into it knowing I was a

single mum, rather than circumstances changing unexpectedly. Surely Jack was a more logical choice for the father of my
child than someone I hadn't yet met? But then, this was *crazy*!
I couldn't just go and have a baby with a platonic, single, gay
friend. Could I? Was it even fair to the baby to bring them into
the world in such unusual circumstances? Under my uncertainty and my nerves, I could feel another emotion. It took me a
moment to realise it was a bubbling of excitement in my belly.
I wanted to do this.

I became aware that I'd been silent for quite a while, Jack
looking at me nervously as I sat with my thoughts. "Annie?" he
finally asked quietly. "I didn't mean to freak you out."

"No, you didn't," I replied, only somewhat dishonestly.
"I'm just thinking about it, that's all. It's not something that
had occurred to me before, but I can't say it doesn't have its
merits." It occurred to me vaguely that I sounded like an English professor, arguing the 'merits' of Jack's suggestion. Georgia
had always teased me about how I became more formal the
more nervous I was, something she had first noticed when I
was asked to present at a staff meeting.

"Well, as long as it has *merits*," Jack grinned, obviously
picking up on the same thing. "Look, I'm not asking you to
decide anything tonight. It's something that's occurred to me
from time to time, but while you were with Adam I dismissed
the whole thing. I'm sure he couldn't have handled you being
pregnant with another man's baby. It would have thrown off his
entire caveman outlook on life." Since the break-up, Jack had
seemingly become willing to unleash four years' worth of negative emotions about Adam which had previously remained under wraps. "But things are different now, so I just thought it

might be something you'd be willing to think about, given the circumstances."

I looked at my long-term friend, ready to tell him that I would think about it; that given more time, I would be able to come to a rational decision about a serious topic. I could discuss it with my family; with my other friends. I opened my mouth to express my thoughts to him, and no one was more surprised than me to hear the words that came out.

"Okay. Let's do it."

# Chapter 9

"You're joking," Jack exclaimed.

It would have been so easy to laugh back, to say "yes! Of course I'm joking! We can't have a baby together!" Even in the moment, I knew that what I said next would determine the entire course of the rest of my life. But I didn't want to joke about it, and I didn't want to take my words back. Of course there was a lot to think about, to talk about, before we made any major life decisions, but what it came down to was this: I wanted a baby. I wanted to have a baby with Jack Delaney. And he wanted to have a baby with me.

"Look," I said slowly, "we obviously need to talk more about it. We can't bring a life into the world based on a five-minute discussion. But yes, you're right. I want a baby, you want a baby. We'd be great parents. You're my closest friend, and I honestly think we could do this together. So... yes, we'll have a proper talk. But I'm serious about wanting to do this, if you are?"

Jack gazed at me for a moment, and I could see the sincerity in his eyes. He nodded. "I think it's time to talk."

WE STAYED UP WELL INTO the night, discussing the matter in detail. We talked about the mechanics of the conception itself – he suggested insemination at home, but I wanted to go straight for IVF. There was no physical contact required, plus a greater chance of success, and keeping the process as clinical as possible seemed easier for me. We discussed our plans for after my maternity leave was up, assuming it all went well – he was sure he could arrange to work a day a week from home, and the rest of the time the baby could go to a family day care run by a friend of his mum's whom Jack had known since he was a kid. We talked about living situations. We agreed we could easily stay in this house, and raise the baby here – Jack would have to give up his home office to create a nursery instead, but that seemed like a small price to pay. Finally, when there was nothing else left to discuss, we got to the topic of relationships.

"What if one of us meets someone after we do this?" Jack asked, the question I had been wondering but hadn't dared to speak out loud.

I shrugged, trying to look more nonchalant than I felt. "Then I guess we meet someone. After all, every second kid nowadays has a step-parent or two, right? And at least in our case, we haven't had the divorce scenario as well. We'd still be co-parents, just with someone else in the picture as well." Even as I said it, a small voice in my head told me I was being naïve. If I had Jack's baby and he met someone, or I did, of course it would change things for both of us – and for the child, too, if they were old enough. Still, one of us hypothetically finding The One somewhere down the track didn't seem like a good enough reason to avoid bringing a life into the world. Every family had their own complications, and besides which, the situation might never happen anyway. It wasn't as if either of us had had much luck in the love department before now.

Part of me felt like the conversation was all a little too easy, that it was ridiculous to make a life-changing decision based on one night of conversation, but then some babies were created after a lot less thought, or no thought at all. We talked for an hour or so longer; well past the point of exhaustion, but I knew I wouldn't have slept even if I'd gone to bed. It's hard to sleep on the night when your life changes.

# Chapter 10

A week later, I had what I quickly and officially decreed to be the worst teaching day I'd ever experienced.

It started when Jacob, one of my more difficult kids, kicked me in the shins – and when I called the office to have him removed, the Assistant Principal acted like I was the grievance rather than the 7-year-old abuser. She came to collect him and he was sent home, but made sure her reluctance to intervene was perfectly evident. Clearly, she didn't like to be pulled away from watching Netflix or scrolling through Facebook or whatever the hell she was doing in her office.

Two hours later, one of my students waved her hand around frantically until I walked over to her. She quickly waved me down and hurriedly whispered "Miss Yates, I farted and a little bit of poo came out."

I closed my eyes. Was it 3 o'clock yet? "Stay there, Jenny," I replied, trying to muster up the last of my patience, while at the same time feeling guilty about my annoyance with a child over what had to be a mortifying situation for her. "Let me call the office." I called the secretary and asked her to ring Jenny's mum, then walked back over to the girl. "Have you got your jumper?" I asked, and when she nodded I instructed her to tie it around her waist and to head straight to the office to go home.

Chalk it up to the temporary insanity that comes with dealing with little people all day, but for some reason it simply never occurred to me to check the chair Jenny had been sitting on. I didn't give it any more thought until an hour later, when another student called me over for help. I bent down to help him with his maths task, but seeing he was going to need more assistance than I'd expected, I pulled out the chair nearest to me, sat down – and froze.

The chair was unmistakeably wet.

I stood up, trying to appear calmer than I actually was, and flew down the hall, where Georgia was reading to her class. "Mind my class," I gasped, tears of shock and humiliation in my eyes.

She stared. "Are you okay? What's happened?" she exclaimed, clearly able to see the stress and disgust painted over my face. I beckoned her over towards the door and whispered "I just... sat... in shit."

Georgia's eyes boggled. "I'm sorry, you *what?*" She seemed amused and disgusted at the same time.

"Oh my God, Georgia, just mind my bloody class!" I hissed. "I'm going to get cleaned up."

Thankfully I had my gym bag in the car, so when I came back I was dressed in my workout gear – not ideal for a professional setting, but a hell of a lot better than a soiled dress! I threw the offending garment in the black bin on my way back in. I didn't think it was something I'd be lining up to wear ever again. A shame, really, considering I'd dressed up especially for school picture day. At least Jenny had the decency to wait until after our pictures were taken, because I wasn't about to pose in my tights and singlet.

I walked through Georgia's room, where she was standing in the adjoining door between our rooms. "What are you doing tonight?" I asked. By now, having recovered from the immediate surprise of seeing me so upset, her lips were twitching with barely restrained amusement. She replied by telling me we were going out to get pissed, which was exactly what I wanted to hear.

CARRIE, GEORGIA AND I had dinner – and multiple cocktails – that night at our favourite Italian place. It wasn't fancy, but their garlic bread was the best I'd ever eaten, and we usually went there every few weeks. Our regular waiter, a good-looking bald guy, knew my order before I gave it. I filled Carrie in on my horrendous day, and the two of them fell about laughing.

"I'm glad you're so amused," I said stiffly.

"Sorry, Annie, but you knew there'd be *shitty* days when you started teaching," Georgia said, and the two of them roared with laughter again. I wondered idly if Georgia had been saving that one since I'd first burst into her classroom that afternoon.

"Yeah, I know you want to *run* away right now," Carrie quipped, "but things will become more *regular* soon."

"You two bitches are so funny," I snapped, but now that the day was getting further away, it was seeming slightly less horrendous and it was hard not to be at least a little amused by my friends' banter. I tried to hide my grin, though.

At that point Georgia either took pity on me or ran out of puns, and decided to offer me some sage advice.

"We're going to invent the official Fallen Oaks Primary Drinking Game," she said solemnly, raising her glass. "It should help us get through the rest of the year, at least."

I started laughing myself then. "We're drinking at work?" I asked, taking a sip of my own cocktail as if to practice. "I'm not sure we'll keep our jobs for too long doing that. Not that I necessarily want to after today, of course."

"We won't drink *at* work," Georgia replied, rolling her eyes. "We'll just keep a bit of a running tally, and then when we get home we'll get smashed."

"I'll write the list," I said, not requiring much convincing. Naturally, as a teacher I had about six pens in my bag. "We take a sip when anyone says 'journey.'"

"And a whole glass every time a meeting is called," Carrie chimed in, grimacing. "We'll need it."

"Okay," I said, scribbling them down on my napkin. "A shot whenever a student swears... and a sip for every parent complaint."

"Oh God," Georgia said good-naturedly. "We'll be pissed in half an hour."

"Okay, so what else? A sip for every time Admin takes a parent's side over us..."

"So again, every time there's a parent complaint," Carrie snorted. "Let's not forget the all-important one, every time a kid doesn't do their homework."

We laughed together as we wrote the list, coming up with a huge variety of reasons to drink. I loved moments like these with my friends; I felt ten years younger than my actual age when we were just being silly together. At the same time, I felt an anxious knot in my stomach when I remembered what I had to tell them tonight. I still hadn't mentioned the baby discussion with Jack, since it wasn't really the sort of thing you brought up in the staffroom. I'd vowed to myself that I would tell them as soon as we were alone together, away from school. Tonight's dinner might have been unplanned before today, but I still knew it was the right time.

It took a bit more liquid courage for me to break the news to them, however. Eventually I took a deep breath and decided to just say it, like ripping off a Band-Aid. "I have some news," I said bluntly. "I've been talking to Jack, and given everything that's happened lately... Well, we're thinking about having a baby."

Silence. It took me a moment to raise my eyes and look at my friends, both of whom were staring back at me, wide-eyed. "A baby?" Carrie repeated slowly. "With... each other?"

"Well, yeah. Neither of us have any romantic prospects, and that obviously wouldn't help Jack even if he did, and we're not getting any younger!" I said, laughing nervously. "We talked it over and it just seems to make sense. Just because we're single doesn't mean we shouldn't get to be parents, too."

Georgia broke the silence. "That's so exciting, Annie! A little baby around again!" she exclaimed. While Georgia's own baby-raising days were well behind her, she still went a little starry-eyed around smaller kids. "Will you have much time off work? Are you guys going to stay living where you are now? Will you do day care or will one of you stay home?"

"Whoa," I laughed, holding up my hand to stop her. "I'm not even pregnant yet, Georgia. I'm glad you're excited, though." I glanced over at Carrie, aware that she'd remained quiet throughout Georgia's burst of energy. "What do you think?"

She smiled. "Congratulations, Annie," she said, but her voice was flat and her smile less than convincing. "A baby!"

I stared at her and raised an eyebrow. "Okay, we've known each other too long for you to get away with that," I replied, trying to keep my tone light. "What do you really think?"

There was an awkward pause as Carrie seemed to try to collect her thoughts. "I just think you're giving up a little bit easily."

I felt as if I'd been slapped. "Giving up easily? How am I giving up? This is what I want. I'm *going after* what I want."

"I'm sorry, Annie. You asked what I think, and I guess I think you should wait for the real deal to come along. There's no saying Adam had to be it for you. Maybe you'll meet Mr Right tomorrow and then you'd be glad you waited for him?"

"Not everyone gets to have your perfect family," I snapped, anger bubbling up inside me now. "Your amazing husband, your two adorable kids. Some of us get a crush on a gay man and a fiancé who cheats on us and leaves us all alone."

The silence that fell now was somehow heavier than the one we'd had before. Once again, it was Georgia who broke it, though tentatively this time. "I thought your crush on Jack was ancient history?" she murmured, looking at me with naked pity.

"Oh, it *is*," I sighed, feeling surprisingly close to tears all of a sudden and not knowing why. "I don't feel that way about him anymore... I wouldn't have sex with him now if you paid me... but, now that Adam's gone, he's the most significant man in my life. Hell, even when Adam was around he was probably *still* the most significant man in my life. It's complicated, that's all." Complicated certainly summed it up. What I had felt for Jack was more real than what I'd felt for most, maybe all, of the other men I'd dated. I'd been deeply besotted with him for the first few months I'd known him, and those feeling didn't go away overnight. For the most part, I knew I was completely over him, and the love I felt for him now was purely platonic; but it wasn't always so easy to see where platonic love ended and romantic love began. I loved Carrie and Georgia as much as any partner, as well; but I was straight, and so were they, so I never had to second guess my feelings for them. With Jack, it was always going to be a bit harder to make the distinction.

I didn't like to think back to when I had feelings for Jack, and most of the time I thought that was because I was still embarrassed about losing my heart to a gay guy. To have been so wrong! Deep down, though, I knew there was a part that was worried that if I thought too much about that time I would invite those feelings back in, opening the floodgates to think about Jack in a way I didn't want to anymore.

"This," Carrie said suddenly, and then paused. "This is why I don't think it's a good idea. You're not even sure on your feelings for the guy and now you want to have a baby with him? Can't you see how much *more* complicated that will make everything?"

"I know my feelings for Jack," I bit back. "He's someone I want in my life for the rest of it, and that sounds to me like a pretty good trait to have in the father of my baby. It's not the 1950s, Carrie! Not every kid has a mum and a dad and a dog in their lives, but that doesn't mean their lives aren't worth living. Look at Georgia, she's doing an amazing job raising Michael!

And at least I'm going into it knowing the status of my relationship with Jack. A lot of women start a family with someone and it fizzles later, causing a massive rift." I paused, collecting my thoughts. "Besides, if I do meet 'Mr Right' tomorrow," I added, adopting a mocking tone as I repeated her term, "maybe we can have a baby down the track too. Jack and I talked about the fact that we might meet someone else. There's no rule saying I can't have more than one kid with more than one man. I wouldn't be the first person to do it. If I find the right man, he'll love me *and* my baby. If he doesn't, he isn't Mr Right, anyway."

There was another pause, and then Carrie nodded slowly. "You're right, Annie," she murmured. "I'm sorry. You just took me by surprise, that's all. It's a big change. I'm sure you'll be an amazing mum, and Jack's a great guy. I'm really happy for you." She leaned over and took my hand. "Honestly." I could see she still wasn't entirely convinced, but she was doing her best to set aside her feelings for my benefit. It was enough for now.

I smiled, feeling as if I was on the verge of tears once more. God, imagine how emotional I would become if I actually did get pregnant? "Thanks, Carrie. Look, it might not even happen yet. There's no point counting our eggs before they're fertilised, right? But whatever happens, I won't be alone. I have more of a support system than a lot of married people do." The three of us shared a smile, then I raised my glass. "And now, let's keep in mind that this might be my last chance for a while to get *totally smashed*!"

# Chapter 11

When I got my appointment for the IVF clinic I arranged the day off for 'medical appointments', avoiding telling my boss exactly what those medical appointments entailed. Before I knew it, Jack and I were in the waiting room. I had my book in front of me and was trying to read, but I couldn't concentrate and kept rereading the same words. Finally I gave up and turned to Jack. "Do you have *any* idea what to expect?" I asked, and he shook his head. I had been planning to look the IVF process up online to get some sort of idea, but Jack had warned me it would be "like using Dr Google – never a good idea". I'd decided he was right and had gone in with no pre-conceived notions (no pun intended), but I was regretting it now. The receptionist had told me over the phone that today was simply a discussion about our medical history and the process, but that didn't stop me feeling nervous. What sort of information would stop the clinic from being willing to go through the IVF process with us? What if the information they gave us about the process going forward made Jack change his mind? What if it made me change mine?

As it turned out, I needn't have worried. The fertility specialist was a relatively young woman who put my mind at ease immediately. She looked over our medical histories, which fortunately didn't raise any red flags, and then talked us through the process. We needed one more consultation after a series of tests and then a counselling session before the treatment began. I had to take hormone injections to get my body to produce more eggs than usual, increasing our odds for success. I also had to get regular blood tests to measure my hormone levels, and scans as it got closer to review how many ovarian follicles I was producing, to find the best time for egg collection. Finally I'd receive a trigger injection to make me ovulate at just the right time, followed by egg collection through day surgery. "All of this, and you just wank into a cup," I murmured to Jack, who laughed quietly. "I guess you could say I *get off* lightly," he smirked. I rolled my eyes in response, trying not to smile.

After the egg collection, of course, would come the egg fertilisation, followed by the embryo transfer – placing the fertilised eggs into my uterus. A little chill ran up my spine when the specialist began talking about this step. It all seemed so real! I had to remind myself that nothing had happened, yet. I didn't want to get ahead of myself.

We made our follow-up appointment time for the following week and walked out to the car. It was only just after midday and we had the rest of the day free, so we decided to see a movie to pass the time. I really didn't take in any of it. My mind was a train hurtling down one track, and I thought that would probably be the case for quite a while yet.

THE PROCESS ALL WENT quite quickly after that. After the standard testing for both of us, followed by our next consultation, and then a relatively pain-free counselling session, we were cleared to go ahead with the IVF process. Having had a lifelong fear of needles the hormone injections and blood tests weren't the most pleasant thing I'd experienced, but they were a price I was willing to pay. It was crazy to think that the baby-making process was so easy for some people and so complicated for others, but at least we had options nowadays. Not so long ago, this whole thing would have been unthinkable.

It was just after the egg collection stage that I received a phone call from an unknown number. I'd been cautious with answering my phone after my break-up with Adam, but that seemed like a lifetime ago now and I had let my guard down. Besides, my first thought was that the call might be connected to the clinic in one way or another. When I answered the phone with a cheery "hello", Adam's voice was the last one I expected to hear.

"Annie," he said softly. "How are you going?"

"Adam?" I tried not to make his name sound like a groan. "I wasn't expecting to hear from you." Briefly, I wondered if he was ringing to tell me he'd made a mistake in ever leaving. I wouldn't have taken him back regardless, but I couldn't deny it would give me a feeling of smug satisfaction to know he thought he'd done the wrong thing.

"Well, I have some news, and I thought it would be best coming from me. Carol – she's the girl I've been seeing –" he had the decency to sound embarrassed at least, even if he didn't come right out and say *the woman I cheated on you with.* "–We're having a baby," he finished, all in a rush.

I could feel the blood drain out of my face. As much as I told myself I didn't care what Adam did with his life, this wasn't exactly welcome news. I pressed my fingers to my temples. "You know I wanted a baby, Adam. Why on earth would you think I would want to hear your happy fucking news?"

"I'm sorry," he mumbled. "I thought you should hear it from me. News spreads, after all, or what if you ran into us on the street? I was only looking out for you, Annie." Now his voice had a whiny tone, enough to set my teeth on edge. *This is why you don't miss him,* a voice in my head reminded me.

"Okay, well, whatever. Congratulations. I'm really happy for you and *Carol,*" I said bitterly. "Anyway, I'm having a baby, too. I thought you should hear it from me. News spreads, after all." The words were out before I knew what I was saying, but I didn't regret saying them. Surely I'd earned the right to be a little petty.

There was a shocked silence on the other end of the line. "You – really? You are? But who –?"

I didn't see the point in mentioning that I wasn't actually pregnant just yet, and although I hated myself for it a little, I decided to have a little fun with his longstanding insecurity about my friendship with Jack. "Oh, you remember Jack? Yeah, I'm having his baby. I knew you'd be really happy for us both. I should invite you to the baby shower!"

Silence. Adam had hung up his end of the line. I grinned to myself as I put my mobile down. Suddenly, answering Adam's call didn't seem like such a bad thing after all.

# Chapter 12

The final stage of the IVF process was a pregnancy test, naturally enough. It was administered two weeks after the embryo transfer and was a nervous wait for me. Jack was with me, and although he tried to keep the atmosphere light I could tell he felt nearly as anxious as I did. When I went for the 7am blood test the clinic assured me they'd ring by 4pm, but that didn't stop me from checking the clock countless times an hour. Jack returned home with me following the test and blasted music as he cleaned the house, trying to keep his mind occupied. I sat with a book in front of me, but it must have taken me twenty minutes to read a single page. I just couldn't take anything in.

When the phone rang it startled us both, even though we'd been thinking of nothing else all day. It was just before 3pm, but it felt like a lifetime had passed since the blood test that morning. I answered the phone with a shaking hand and a trembling voice. "Hello, Annabel speaking," I murmured. I kept it on loudspeaker so Jack could hear what she had to say, but I didn't dare look at him. I felt entirely responsible if the attempt had failed, even though I knew that was nonsensical.

"Annabel! It's Samantha here from the clinic. How are you?" she asked, which seemed a ridiculous question considering *how I was* depended entirely on what she had to tell me. She seemed to realise that herself, because she went on without waiting for an answer. "I thought you'd like to know that your procedure was successful."

The rest of the phone conversation passed in a blur – she might as well have been speaking Greek. I wasn't sure I even managed to get a full sentence out, but the one thing I do remember was turning to look at Jack's face. His expression mirrored what mine had to show – a shocked kind of amazement. Awe, excitement, and terror were all fighting inside me for dominance.

I hung up the phone and stared, stunned, into space, trying to get my thoughts together. I was *pregnant*. It hardly seemed possible. I tried to tell myself to be cool – it was still early days, and there was no guarantee it would all go smoothly and actually result in a baby – but my mind was whirring, my heart racing, and I couldn't hold back my excitement if I tried.

Jack swooped in and hugged me, and I held on more tightly than usual. We were going to be parents! As he held me I felt myself getting teary. I tried to imagine telling the Annie of ten years ago that my friendship with Jack would end up leading to this.

Jack and I had always loved asking each other hypothetical questions - would you rather live forever, or die tomorrow? Would you rather watch *Die Hard* (our favourite movie) every day for the rest of your life, or never again, to keep it special? If you had to choose between books and television, which would you choose? Our answers were usually opposite to each other – I chose to live forever, watch *Die Hard* every day, and give up

TV for books, and he chose the other option every time – but it didn't stop our enthusiasm for the game.

This felt like one of our hypotheticals come to life – would you rather have a lifelong platonic friendship, or the family you've always dreamed of? – the difference being, in this case we didn't have to choose. We could have it all.

# Chapter 13

I knew the girls probably expected my news when I suggested we go out for dinner the following night, but neither one said anything. We sat down and ordered, and when I asked for a lemonade instead of anything alcoholic I could feel their eyes on me expectantly.

"Well, ladies," I said when the waiter had gone, "I've brought you here for a reason tonight." I wiggled my eyebrows up and down, trying to create an air of mystery, even though I knew they would know full well what I was going to say. "I'm going to be a Mum!"

The girls erupted into cheers. I watched Carrie's face to see if she looked genuinely happy for me and was gratified to see that she did. I knew she still had her private misgivings about the situation, but I was quietly confident that she'd come around when the baby was born, if not before.

The girls bubbled over with questions. When was I due? Did I have any gut instincts about the sex of the baby? Would I find out when I could? Was Jack as excited as I was? Had I told my parents or my sister yet?

I laughed and answered all of their questions as fully and honestly as I could. No, I didn't really have a preference about the sex – any baby at all was a blessing! – but my mental image was of us with a little boy, a mini Jack. I thought we would probably find out but I hadn't checked with Jack yet, and I wasn't interested in knowing if he didn't, because I couldn't possibly keep that secret for months! Yes, Jack was just as over-the-moon as I was, and no, neither of us had told our families yet. My parents didn't even know it was a possibility, and I wasn't sure how they would take it. I tried not to let the thought of our difficult conversation to come darken my mood.

My friends and I talked over the baby issue for what felt like an hour, but I couldn't get enough of it. I had been a part of baby conversations so many times before, and although I was always happy for my friends, a large part of me was envious at not being the one sharing the exciting news myself. I couldn't be happier now my dream was finally coming true!

"Well, I have some news, too," Georgia offered when our excited chatter had finally died down. "I'm seeing someone."

"No way!" I exclaimed. Although Georgia had been casually dating since her separation, this was the first time she'd actually made any kind of serious announcement about anyone. "Tell us everything!"

She grinned, looking like the cat that had got the cream. "His name is Ryan, he's stupidly hot, and he's 25."

"25!" Carrie squealed. "How did you guys meet?"

"Remember the work party my friend Monica dragged me along to? Well, I met him there and we had a bit of a kiss. We were both pretty pissed, so I didn't think I'd hear from him again, but he got my number off Monica and we ended up going out. We've been out a few times now, so I think something might actually be happening."

"Slept with him?" Carrie cut right to the chase.

"Yes, but *not* until the fourth date," Georgia said, and we rewarded her statement by oohing like schoolgirls. Georgia had barely made it to a second date with any of the guys she'd hooked up with since Scott left, so restraining herself sexually with this guy just might be a good sign. "Want to see a photo?" Without waiting for an answer, she showed us his Facebook profile pic. I stared at the photo, open-mouthed. "He's *divine!*" I exclaimed. "Well done, Georgia!"

"I know he's way too hot for me," she said a little shyly, "but I think he has a bit of a thing for curvy women. Or for older women. Or both."

Carrie furrowed her brow. "It's great you've met someone, and trust me, you're gorgeous and you well and truly deserve him! – but are you at all worried about that? Like it's a... fetish thing for him?"

Georgia laughed. "Honey, I'm ten years older than him, he looks like a frigging movie star, and he goes down on me like it's an Olympic sport. I think he can have whatever fetish he wants."

I raised my glass. "Cheers to that!" I exclaimed, and the three of us were soon laughing again.

# Chapter 14

I messaged my parents and my sister and asked to have dinner at Mum and Dad's the following night. They were all free and although my requesting a family get-together was fairly unusual, they all just said how nice it would be to catch up. I mulled over the idea of Jack coming along as well, but decided against it. If they weren't thrilled with the idea of the pregnancy Jack's presence would temper their responses, but it would just mean we'd have to have it out another time. It was better to get it all over and done with as soon as possible. I know not many people treat the idea of telling their family about their pregnancy with so much trepidation, but when you're not even in a relationship, it's not the easiest conversation to have. I was beginning to wish I'd told them we were planning to go the IVF route, to make breaking this news easier on me, but it was too late now.

I felt instantly more at ease when I arrived at Mum and Dad's familiar home and gave their Labrador Rufus a cuddle at the front door. I might not visit my parents as often as I should have, but their place still felt like home to me, warm and cosy. I gave them each a hug, holding on a little bit tighter than usual, but not enough to alarm them. I decided to wait until Julie arrived before I said anything, so I just told them my latest work stories and politely refused the red wine Dad offered me, saying I felt like something lighter and accepting a sparkling water in its place.

It felt like an eternity before Julie arrived, twenty minutes late as usual. When we'd served up our roast and sat at the table together, I decided it was now or never. I took a deep breath and said simply, "I have some news".

They all turned to look at me, mild curiosity on their faces. I think they were expecting a work-related announcement, something benign like changing to a new school. Instead, I launched into the story, getting it over with as quickly and as bluntly as I could.

"Since Adam and I broke up, I've been feeling a bit more of a pull to have a baby. I was starting to think it wouldn't happen, but then Jack started talking to me about the same kind of feelings. Long story short..." I paused, took another intake of breath. "...We've gone through an IVF cycle. I'm having a baby!"

With my monologue finished, I looked around at their faces for the first time, taking in their expressions. Julie's eyebrows were raised, her jaw slightly opened, in an almost comical expression of surprise. My Dad's jaw was clenched, and Mum's eyes were filling lightly with tears. I had only a brief moment to wonder whether they were tears of happiness or sadness before she broke the silence.

"Oh, sweetheart... congratulations," she said, but her voice was soft and hesitant. "This is... well, this is a bit of a surprise." She looked to Dad, as if for help. He cleared his throat before taking over. "Are you sure this is what you want?" he asked, his voice hoarse.

"Well, it's a bit late now," I said, a lame attempt at a joke. When I saw alarm cross Mum's face, I mentally kicked myself. "No! I mean, it is what I want. I was just kidding. This is what I want, really," I added, hearing a pleading note come into my voice. "I wouldn't have done it without thinking it through."

"It's not that we're not happy for you," Mum said, the tears still threatening. "It's just not what we expected for you. We wanted you to have the fairytale, baby girl. The whole thing." Now I could feel a lump in my throat, and I knew tears were starting to form in my own eyes as well. I had known it would be a bit of a shock for my parents, but I'd expected a happier reaction about the impending birth of their first grandchild. My parents, my friends – would *everyone* think this baby was a mistake? Would Jack and I love him or her enough for it not to matter? And, worst of all, had I disappointed them?

Julie had been uncharacteristically quiet, letting Mum and Dad do all the talking. Suddenly, to my surprise, she broke in. "Well, I think it's *great,*" she said, putting one arm around me and squeezing me fiercely. "Congratulations, Annie! You'll be a natural as a mum. You'll love every bit of it, I can tell. And Jack will be an amazing dad! Who cares if it's not the 'fairytale'? How many people get that nowadays, anyway? There are no guarantees these days."

I looked at my sister, surprised and moved by her enthusiasm and her loyalty towards me. Particularly given her own thoughts towards having kids, I hadn't expected such unreserved happiness for me when she heard my news. Now the tears that had been threatening finally spilled out of my eyes. I wasn't normally the weepy type, but maybe the hormones had already set in, or maybe this was just how much it all meant to me. "Thank you, Julie," I said, smiling gratefully at her. "Aunty Julie," I added for good measure, which made her laugh and throw her arms around me again. I knew she would make an amazing aunt.

I looked at my parents then. "And Grandma and Grandad," I added, my voice thick with emotion. "Are you going to support us? This is your first grandbaby, after all."

It was my Dad who spoke first. "Annie, we'll always support you, you know that. This might not have been what we hoped for and expected for you, but you're our daughter and we love you. We obviously want what's best for you, and we'll help out in any way we can."

I smiled. I could see they still had their misgivings, but all I really needed was their support. Over time, I hoped, their doubts would go away, and their love for their grandchild would only grow stronger.

# Chapter 15

I had always had romantic notions of pregnancy. Of course I knew from Carrie and some other friends that the reality didn't really match up to my preconceived ideas, but I still loved the idea of having a large, round stomach – well, larger, rounder and more socially acceptable than my current one, anyway! I imagined myself gliding around in long, flowing dresses while people remarked on how I was glowing.

The reality was very, very different.

Firstly, and most grievously, I'd never been so sick in my life. Morning sickness didn't begin to cover the nausea that followed me around all day, although yes, my actual vomiting did seem to be fairly limited to early mornings, which was lucky at least for work. My day was spent munching on salty crackers, trying to keep the sickness at bay. I was also gassy in a way I'd never imagined, and rather than glowing, I just seemed to sweat. My face was bloated up like a puffer fish all the time, not to mention my ankles! My boobs had never looked so good before, but they'd also never been sorer, and I was suddenly glad no one wanted to touch them. I hoped the first trimester was the worst of it, but I wasn't so sure. I bought all the usual books, including some on audiobook for those days when I just couldn't even be bothered to hold a hard copy up to my face.

Reading them confirmed that I was normal, but it didn't really help matters. In my current state, my misery was too great to love anything at all, even company. I kept telling myself that it would all be worthwhile in the end, and I knew it would be, but it was still going to be a very long nine months.

My parents had come around to the idea and Mum had even started shopping, rather pre-emptively in my opinion. We could find out the sex at ten weeks, due to a new blood test they had available, but Jack and I had yet to agree on whether we wanted to. I wanted to get organised, thanks to the teacher in me; he wanted to have a surprise. I kept telling him the surprise would be whether I made it through the labour in one piece. He was willing to acquiesce to my preference, since as he so delicately put it I was the one 'suffering through the pregnancy', but I wanted to convince him it was the right decision, rather than forcing him into it. And so, as the ten-week timeframe approached, we were still undecided about whether we would find out.

"Blame the nesting instinct," I told Jack on the Saturday before our Tuesday appointment. "I just want to get a nice little home ready for him or her, and it's a lot easier to do if we know the sex. I don't want to paint a nursery green."

"What if we have more than one?" Jack countered, and I looked up in surprise, my hand frozen in mid-air on my copy of *What to Expect When You're Expecting.* "I'm sorry, what?"

Jack looked suddenly sheepish. "I just meant, maybe in the future we'll have another. I mean, I'm not expecting that, but you never know, right? So we'll want some kind of neutral nursery, just in case."

I continued staring at my friend, at a loss for words. It was a natural enough suggestion, I supposed, but I'd actually never considered having more than one child with Jack. This one felt like a miracle, and even though I'd expected to have a bundle of them when I was marrying Adam, it seemed like I should just be grateful for what I had here. The fact that Jack was thinking further into the future was very interesting indeed.

"I didn't mean to freak you out," Jack laughed, sounding like he was making an effort to sound casual. "One baby is just fine by me."

I found my voice. "I'm not arguing with you," I reassured him. "I'm just... surprised. I never would have thought of having more than one, but it's definitely something I'm open to in the future. Let's have the first one first! I guess we'll just wait and see what happens?" My voice went up at the end, expressing my uncertainty. Jack nodded and smiled. "We'll wait and see," he confirmed. "Just like we'll do about the sex..."

I laughed. "Nice try."

I was determined to get my way, right up until we were sitting in the waiting room. My heart was thumping in my chest, terrified of what they were going to say. I knew it was too early to find out about some abnormalities or complications, but there was a definite chance of hearing about some of them, or even miscarriage. I didn't realise I was trembling until Jack put his hand gently on my arm. "You okay, Yates?" he asked softly.

I forced a smile as I looked back at him. "I'm fine, aside from the fact that I'm more scared than I've ever been before," I laughed softly, trying to make light of it.

He pulled me in for a sideways hug. "I know, honey, but it's okay. Chances are, the baby's perfectly healthy. If the worst happens, we'll get through it together."

"I don't want to find out the sex," I blurted out.

Jack looked at me in surprise. "I thought you were gung-ho about that?" He still wasn't happy with the idea, but had told me it was my decision in the end. "You're the one doing all the heavy lifting, after all," he had said during our last discussion. "If you want to find out, we can find out."

I shook my head mutely. Sitting here, scared to death that the scan was going to find something wrong with the unborn baby I'd already fallen in love with, I realised the sex was completely irrelevant. All I wanted was a healthy child. Besides, I had so much love for the man sitting beside me, the man who had made this all possible. The man who even now, while he must be as nervous as I was, was focussed only on comforting me. If Jack wanted to wait to find out what we were having, well, it seemed like the least I could do for him.

I'll admit that I left with a slight twinge of disappointment about not knowing what I was having, but it was nothing compared to the elation I felt after the test revealed that all was well. The baby was healthy! This was really happening! I knew nothing was ever certain, but I had a sudden feeling of calmness. This was all going to work out.

Jack smiled at me as we walked out. "Are you sure you made the right choice?" he asked, and I knew he was referring to my decision to wait on finding out the sex.

I returned his smile. "Absolutely," I said. "There's only one thing I'm worried about, and that's keeping this little nugget healthy. It doesn't matter if it's a mini me or a mini you."

Jack wrapped his arms around me and kissed me gently on the forehead. Right then and there, walking along in the cool evening air, everything was just perfect.

# Chapter 16

I waited until the three-month mark to tell my workplace about the pregnancy. I wasn't sure how they would react, especially being unmarried. It shouldn't matter in this modern age, but as a 'role model' for children I thought it could have been an issue. As it turned out, I needn't have worried. My boss Ann-Marie was completely understanding, possibly partially as a result of having a gay brother. I think she could understand my story at least from Jack's perspective, if not my own. She congratulated me and then told me I could work as long as I wanted and we'd sort out maternity leave and all the other technicalities later on. I was due in February, which meant I would finish up the current school year and not go back. I wouldn't have to worry about who my replacement was or do any kind of handover of the class. I hadn't planned it that way, but it was ideal. At this stage my plan was to have just the one school year off and then go back, but I wasn't sure if that would work once I had the reality of a squirming baby in my arms. Financially, though, it might be our only option. Who could afford to stay home for long in this day and age?

It was a tradition at my workplace to present banana bread to announce your pregnancy. No one really knew where the tradition started, but it had carried on from year to year despite the high turnover of staff at our school. I came in early the day after I told Ann-Marie my news and placed the banana bread on the staffroom table while the room was still empty, to let them have the fun of gossiping about who the bearer of good news might be. I heard several names came up, and eventually mine, but in a sort of joking way. Everyone knew I was single and didn't consider me a viable prospect for this kind of news.

It felt like an eternity before first break rolled around, even though the first session of the day was only two hours long. Even while I was teaching, all I could picture was my lunchtime announcement. As it turned out, one of my students' lunchboxes went missing and by the time I made it over to the staffroom, a dozen teachers, most of the ones not on duty, were already there. All heads turned as I walked through the door, as I knew from past experience that they did for every arrival on banana bread day. Carrie was already in there, keeping quiet. "Is it you?" one of the teacher aides called out from the back of the room as I came through the door. I'd been there long enough to know this was the standard question asked of everyone on banana bread day, so they didn't necessarily suspect it was actually mine. I had planned on playing it cool, but a huge grin broke out on my face. "It's me!" I confirmed, to cheers and whoops of delight. A few of the older women on staff rushed to hug me, and when I sat down I was regaled with congratulations. I knew some of them would be dying to know who the father was, but they were all too tactful to pose the question, and I didn't want to get into it right now. For one moment, I just wanted it to be about me.

THE PREGNANCY SYMPTOMS did ease after the first trimester, fortunately enough, and the next few months passed in a happy blur. We decided to do a soft lilac colour for the baby's room, perfect for either a boy or a girl, and, between Mum and I, we were soon stocking up on all the necessities. Jack helped out where he could, of course, but buying baby furniture wasn't really his forte. One day when Mum came over to help wash and fold some of the baby's linen, she hit me with a question I hadn't expected. "Isn't Jack going to contribute financially to the baby's room?" she asked, not looking up from folding a tiny yellow blanket.

I frowned. "Well, this isn't really his thing, you know. I'm much more interested in the nursery side of things." I paused. "Besides, if we were a couple you wouldn't be expecting us each to buy equal shares of things."

Mum sighed. "I know, Annie, but the point is you're *not* a couple. You've each got your own money and I don't want to see you going broke paying for the baby while he's living on easy street."

"Mum!" I snapped, frustration rising in my chest. "I'm not *going broke*. I *like* buying things for the baby. I'm sure Jack will help out when the time comes." As I said it, I realised we hadn't really discussed the financial side of things with each other. I had just assumed Jack would help out, but we didn't really have any kind of proper plan in place.

The worst thing about mothers – or at least my mother – is no matter how annoying and out-of-touch you think their comments are at the time, they stay with you and plant a seed in your brain.

That night, when Jack came home, I decided to broach the topic with him. "Mum said something interesting today," I said in as casual a voice as I could muster.

"Your mother always says interesting things," Jack snorted. He and Mum got on quite well, but he wasn't immune to the fact that she could be a little intrusive at times.

"Well, this was about us," I said, which had the effect of making Jack look up from his phone. "Us?" he asked, frowning. "You and her, or you and me?"

"You and me," I confirmed. "She mentioned how you haven't bought any baby furniture yet. It totally doesn't bother me," I rushed to add, seeing Jack's expression change. "I know baby furniture isn't really your area of interest, and that's fine! It just made me think that maybe we should make some kind of a financial plan. I mean, we'll have things like clothes and food and nappies to worry about straight away, but later on we need to decide if we want to help out with its first car, or maybe if we want to do private school, or whatever. If we were a traditional couple we'd obviously have joint finances, so I just want to make sure we're covered. Especially while I'm on maternity leave," I added nervously. I did receive some maternity pay, but it wouldn't cover my full wage for the whole time I was off, especially if I decided to stay home for longer than a year. I didn't want to leech off Jack for that time, but realistically I would need some kind of assistance. I was kicking myself for not thinking of this sooner. What the hell would I do if Jack turned around and refused to help out financially?

Of course, I needn't have worried. Jack wasn't the type. He was shaking his head before I even finished my sentence. "You don't have to worry about that, babe. I mean, I'm a little pissed off that you don't just know I'd help you out, honestly," he added, and I could see in his deep blue eyes that he was serious – uncharacteristically so. Jack was the most even-tempered guy I knew. "Do you think I'm some kind of deadbeat dad? I would have thought you'd have known me long enough to think better of me than that."

"I'm sorry," I blurted out. "I'm just not used to being vulnerable, financially. I mean, even with Adam I had my own finances on top of our joint ones."

"That's what we'll do, then," said Jack simply.

I frowned at him, not following. "What's what we'll do?"

"We'll set up a joint bank account. We can each put, say, 10% of our wages in there, or $200 a fortnight, or whatever works. Whatever we need, I don't really know. But, that's the account for this little nugget in here." He gestured towards my growing belly. "Then we'll have most of our wage for ourselves, and you can do with that whatever you want, but baby stuff comes out of our joint account. We could even set up two joint accounts and have one for long-term savings for the kid." He shrugged as if he was open to anything.

I thought about it and couldn't come up with any argument against it. I nodded slowly. "Yeah, that should work." I smiled at Jack, relieved, wondering why I'd ever let myself get so worked up about it in the first place.

# Chapter 17

When I was just shy of seven months along Georgia, Carrie and I went out to dinner again. I'd started hibernating a bit, finding it more and more difficult to get up the motivation to take my bloated stomach out on girls' nights. I was so tired at the end of the working day that I just wanted to go home and put my feet up. It was Carrie who insisted on another dinner, our first in three months. The three of us had let our friendship slip a little, and I knew a large part of that was my fault – although Georgia shared some of the blame, given she was still on a high with her toyboy. We obviously still saw each other at work, but given the nature of teaching and lunchtime duties there were whole days when we didn't see each other at all, except for maybe ten minutes in the staffroom in the morning or afternoon. "It's not *quality* time together," Carrie said when she suggested the dinner, "and God knows you won't be having much quality time with us when that little bugger comes along." I wasn't offended, knowing she was as excited about the baby as I was. Despite her initial misgivings, Carrie had already started plotting and planning for my baby and was even in charge of throwing me a baby shower, a job she'd gleefully volunteered for. It was going to be next month at Carrie's place and she'd started making plans and buying decorations –

I had given her a budget, but I knew she was putting in far more of her own money and doing it as a real labour of love.

It was a Saturday night only one week before the end of the school year when the three of us slid into a table at our regular Italian place. "So, how's things?" Carrie asked both of us after we'd ordered.

I answered first. "I'm swollen, I'm uncomfortable, but I'm happy," I said honestly. "I wouldn't have thought weighing roughly the same size as an elephant could be this enjoyable. It's tough, but it's all good." I smiled, resting one hand on my belly and feeling a satisfying, gentle kick in return.

Georgia went then, having something a bit more exciting than bloating to talk about. "Things with Ryan are still going really well," she gushed. "He's such a prince. We've been going out for over six months, can you believe it?"

"What I can't believe," I said, pouring a drink of water, "is that you've been going out this long and we haven't met this prince yet."

Georgia giggled coyly. "It's just that he's so young," she said. "I don't want him to–"

"Meet your old maiden friends and be scared off?" Carrie asked dryly.

"No!" Georgia protested, even though I suspected there was a hint of truth to it. "I don't want him to feel out of sorts or something. I mean, will you guys have anything to talk to him about?"

"Do *you*?" Carrie countered. "You're just about our age too, you know."

Georgia looked abashed. "Of course, I should introduce you. I just wasn't sure if you would want to. I'll arrange it!"

"Okay, guilt trip over," Carrie said. "Tell us all about this wonderful young'un you've got yourself."

Georgia's face lit up once more as she filled us in on Ryan's personality, his witty sense of humour and of course, his prowess and stamina in bed. "I tell you," she said, "once you go young, you never go..." She paused, stumped. We all tried to think of a clever end to her sentence. "Unfun?" I offered.

She shrugged. "I feel like we could do better than that, but sure! Unfun. I can honestly see this being a long-term thing," she added, to my surprise. I knew Georgia was smitten with Ryan, but I hadn't really thought of it being anything serious. She seemed to be having so much fun with him, and given the age difference I had put it down to just that: fun. Of course, if the man was older we wouldn't think twice about it, so maybe I wasn't giving the situation a chance.

Carrie looked as surprised as I felt, but she recovered quickly. "That's fantastic, George! Can we be bridesmaids at your wedding?" she teased, and Georgia laughed. "I don't think we'll get *that* far ahead of ourselves," she said, shaking her head. "To be honest, I'm not sure if I'll ever get married again."

"Really?" Carrie asked, surprised. "You're not interested?"

Georgia shrugged. "Never say never, but I've been down that road and it didn't work out so well, so why would I put myself through that again? I don't know. I guess it depends if I meet the right guy."

"Well, you're still one better than I am," I said after a slightly awkward pause. "I'm not sure if I'll ever get married at all." To my surprise, I felt a slight twinge as I said it. I thought the marriage dream had died when Adam left me, but maybe it meant more to me than I thought. My feelings must have shown on my face, because when I looked up I saw my friends staring at me with naked sympathy.

"You never know what lies ahead, Annie," Carrie said softly, putting one hand over mine. "The right guy could be just around the corner."

"That's right! Or, maybe you don't get married. Who cares? You've got us, right? And Jack. And your family. And little bub here. You have more than enough to be grateful for," Georgia added with a smile.

"Of course!" I laughed, trying to make my voice sound lighter than I felt. "Of course, it'll work out one way or the other. It's just..." I paused, trying to put my thoughts into words. "Don't get me wrong, I'm beyond grateful for this opportunity. But I do wonder if maybe Mr Right *is* just around the corner, or *was* just around the corner... do you think he'd be turned off? I mean, I'm not in the most conventional situation. Most guys probably don't want to raise someone else's child, especially when the dad is your gay buddy. I just would hate to think that I'd find the right person and lose him because of this whole thing."

Carrie shook her head fiercely. "If he's the right person he'll love you *and* the baby. He won't be scared off, if it's meant to be. And if he is, you're better off without him!"

"That's right," Georgia agreed. "Wouldn't you rather have the baby you've dreamt of for so long, rather than some guy who's going to be scared and run off because you happen to have a child? A hell of a lot of people our age are divorced with kids. If anything, your situation is easier for a guy to come into because he doesn't have to deal with some deranged ex. Jack is a great guy, and he's so easy to get along with!"

"Best case scenario, you end up with both – the baby and the man," Carrie said. "Worst case scenario, you end up with the baby and you're single. Either way, I think you're pretty damn lucky."

I nodded, smiled and told my friends they were right, and I knew, of course, that they were. But it didn't stop one small part of me from wondering.

# Chapter 18

As any teacher can attest, there is no day quite like the last day of the school year. By the time you get there, between report cards, parent-teacher interviews, cleaning out your classroom, creating portfolios and everything else that goes into Term 4, you feel like you've run a marathon. You're mentally and physically exhausted, but also unspeakably excited about the six weeks off to come. If you're one of the more sentimental teachers (like Georgia, Carrie and myself), you're also teary, saying goodbye to your own class as well as the departing teachers. For most teachers, there is only one suitable response to all of the mixed emotions that come with the end of the school year: you get drunk. This year that wasn't an option for me, so I decided to self-medicate with cake instead, while my colleagues whooped and danced all around me. I'd opted to head into the city with them despite my pregnancy, but I was regretting it. The urge to be at home in my pyjamas was almost overwhelming. Still, I reminded myself, I had nearly two months off before my baby was due, and I would get plenty of quality pyjama time then. I might as well take the time now to celebrate the end of another school year.

One of my colleagues slid into the bench beside me, a woman about ten years older than me who taught Year 5 with

Georgia. I had never had much to do with Felicia, but I knew Georgia found her slightly overbearing (or, as George put it, "a massive pain in my rear end"). "How's it going, Annie?" Felicia asked, nodding towards my glass of sparkling water. "Not quite the same as getting on the piss, is it?"

I laughed politely, even though Felicia always put me slightly on edge. "Not quite, but it's a small price to pay," I said, my standard response when anyone asked a question along those lines. I had always thought it was strange how parents felt the need to say "but of course I love them!" or "it's *so* worthwhile, though!" whenever they complained about their children's behaviour, and here I was, doing the same kind of thing before I was even a mum.

"Of course!" Felicia exclaimed, having four kids of her own and being no stranger to the world of mummy guilt. "I'm so excited for you and your... friend. John, isn't it?"

"Jack," I corrected. I had filled a few staff members in on the paternity of the baby several months ago and let the word spread through the staff. It had seemed the easiest way to go about it and obviously, I was right.

"Of course," Felicia said again. "Are you and Jack organised? The plan is to live together as one big happy family, isn't it?"

"Yes," I said, trying not to let my irritation show. "That's the plan."

"Oh, good! It would bother me, living with a man I wasn't in a relationship with. I'm so glad it doesn't bother you," she purred. I smiled tightly, wondering if this woman had been named the poster child of Passive-Aggression or something. "So is the nursery ready? Have you picked a name yet?" She held her hands up as if in surrender. "Not that I'm asking to know it, of course!" she added with a hearty laugh. "I know, better than many, how one likes to keep these things secret."

Now my pyjamas and slippers were calling me more fiercely than before. I took a large sip of my sparkling water before answering. "We're pretty organised with the furniture and everything," I confirmed, "but we haven't actually talked names yet. I mean, we don't know the sex or anything," I added, when I saw the look of surprise cross her face.

"Oh, but *still!* You can at least come up with a shortlist of names for each!" she exclaimed. The truth was, I had floated a couple of my favourites to Jack and he'd looked less than impressed, so we'd never really come back to it. "It's on the list of things to do," I said instead, smiling tightly at my co-worker. Where the hell were my friends, anyway? I craned my neck but couldn't see any sign of Carrie, and Georgia seemed to be dirty dancing with Jim, the occupational therapist. I was stuck.

"I hope that list isn't too long!" Felicia chuckled. "What are you, seven months along? You look ready to pop already! I know two months might *seem* like a long time, but actually it'll go like that." She snapped her fingers. "Don't forget you might go early, of course. I made the mistake of thinking I had a long time with my first, but not with my second or my third or –"

I'd officially had enough. "Excuse me," I said to Felicia, trying to look as sickly as possible. "I'm not feeling the best."

"Oh!" Felicia leapt to her feet, clearly trying to avoid ending up with vomit all over her dress. "Of course! Go!"

I rushed off towards the bathroom to keep up appearances. The baby was pushing on my bladder a bit anyway. When I'd finished in there, I came out and hunted around for Carrie, trying to avoid looking in Felicia's direction. I breathed a sigh of relief when I saw my friend, leaning against the wall as she talked to her fellow Year 3 teacher. I rushed over to them and joined in their conversation, all the while doing maths in my head as to exactly how long I needed to stick around before I could go home and still look somewhat sociable. Jack, bless his heart, had offered to come and get me whenever I wanted, so that I could avoid parking in the city. I sent him a quick message and he replied saying he was on his way.

"Does everyone ask you stupid, intrusive questions about the baby?" I asked him on the way home.

"Like what?" Jack laughed and I quickly filled him in on my conversation with Felicia, adopting a shrill voice for her side of the conversation. I included liberal use of the term "of course!", even more than she'd used herself. I liked to think my accents and impressions were top-notch, although I secretly knew the reality didn't quite match up to my interpretation.

"Well, she sounds obnoxious," Jack said dryly when I had finished. "She just sounds like a busybody. I wouldn't let her get to you. But no, in answer to your question, I don't really get too many intrusive questions. Actually, for the most part, people seem to forget about the baby at my work. I think because I don't have a wife who's expecting it doesn't feel real to people."

I gestured to my stomach. "This is real, trust me. People are stupid," I grimaced. "But lucky you. It's not much fun having to answer all those questions."

"That's fair, they are." He paused, and then added, "I kind of hate that no one talks to me about it, though. They obviously don't think I'm as important as the women at work who are pregnant, or the guys whose partners are having a baby. It's really not cool," he said, an uncharacteristic rant from my normally light-hearted friend.

"I guess I haven't thought about it from your perspective," I admitted. "That must suck, too. It's pretty unfair."

He shrugged. "It's unimportant, in the long run. We still get our baby and even if my workmates don't think it's 'real', I still get my *real* paternity leave to spend quality time with you and the kid."

"Speaking of 'the kid'," I said, "we really *should* talk about names."

"Actually, I was thinking we need to talk about surnames," he said. When I looked at him quizzically he said "I was assuming we'd have a little Delaney in there, but I'm not sure what your thoughts are."

"Oh!" It was another issue I hadn't given any thought to. It was alarming, how many of those little matters were arising. I briefly wondered what else I hadn't thought about. "Um, I guess I thought it would be a Yates. I mean, I'm–" I stopped myself before saying *I'm the one doing all the work.* "I'm one of two girls," I said lamely. "I don't see why I can't carry on the family name. Or hyphenated, maybe? Delaney-Yates. Yates-Delaney. Whatever sounds better. Delaney-Yates, I think. Yates-Delaney sounds like a yoghurt or something," I mused. "Delaney-Yates is like a law firm. Sophisticated." I stopped rambling when I saw the look on Jack's face. He was visibly wincing. "I've never really been a fan of hyphenated names," he explained.

I felt frustration rising up in my chest. "Then what? We flip a coin? We have to pick one sooner or later. It's the 21$^{st}$ Century. We don't have to give the baby your name just because *you're* the man. This is my baby, too."

Jack sighed. "We're nearly home. Let's put this on hold for now."

I looked out the window. "Fine," I muttered, and the rest of the car ride home was silent.

# Chapter 19

Carrie had arranged my baby shower for the following weekend – a week into holidays to give her time to get her house cleaned and everything prepared, but early enough to not interfere with the Christmas season. When I arrived at her place to help set up, I was blown away by the gorgeous scene, all lilacs and yellows everywhere. Amazing cupcakes with pink and blue icing were laid out on a high tea plate on the table and balloons were placed all around the room. "It looks gorgeous, Carrie!" I squealed, touched by my friend's efforts.

"Only the best for you! Have a punch," she offered, directing me to a seat. "I know you came early to help set up, but everything's organised. I thought we could have some quiet time before everyone arrives." Her husband had taken the kids out for the day, despite Aria's best efforts to stay and join in on the party, so her house was unusually peaceful.

I smiled as I sank gratefully into the seat. "That sounds fantastic," I told her. "Thank you so much for everything."

She waved my thanks away and ladled out a glass of punch for each of us. "Cheers," she said, raising her glass. "To a happy and healthy baby, and to fantastic bloody holidays!"

"I'll drink to that," I laughed. "I love teaching and all, but this really is the best time of year."

"Oh, I don't know," she said, deadpan. "I'll really miss the six am alarm. Of course, you'll think six is a sleep-in, soon!"

I grimaced. As much as I was looking forward to motherhood, I really wasn't sure how I would cope with the lack of sleep. "Please don't remind me," I begged. "I'm a strictly eight-hours-a-night-minimum girl."

"Not for long," she teased. "Don't worry, you'll learn to cope. That's why babies are cute, you know; so you don't resent them when they wake you up every night. It's an evolutionary thing or something, to stop you killing them."

"So everyone says," I grumbled. Then, wanting to change the subject away from terrifying reality for a moment, I asked about her plans for the holidays. It was something we'd already discussed at length to get us through the hectic last few weeks of school, but Carrie's face still lit up as she discussed the family trip to the Sunshine Coast she was taking in January. I had felt slightly envious of Carrie's family situation for so long that I felt a familiar twinge before reminding myself that I, too, would soon be able to take family trips away. I was sure Jack would be up for joining us but even if it was just me and the baby, that would be wonderful, too.

Time passed quickly and soon enough guests started trickling in. My Mum and Julie were amongst the first to arrive, followed by a mixture of my cousins, some closer workmates (no Felicia in sight, fortunately) and some other friends of mine from outside of work. Carrie's living room was soon filled with happy chatter and laughter.

"Okay, let's play some games!" Carrie's voice rang out when everyone was settled. "We'll start with the tape measure game." I looked at her in horror; this was one we hadn't discussed. "For those who don't know, you're each going to cut a piece of string the size you think Annie's stomach is. Then we'll measure it against her and the closest person gets a prize!" She gestured towards a row of small polka-dotted party bags that adorned the table, prizes for all the different games.

I grimaced. Having people estimate my general size and weight was never exactly the top of my to-do list, and I was surprised Carrie had decided on this game without discussing it with me first. Still, I was a good sport and kept my mouth shut, even when some people cut pieces of string large enough to go around the average killer whale.

After that we played a variety of less controversial games, and after stuffing my face full of cupcakes all afternoon it was time to open presents. Most people gave me baby things of varying levels of usefulness. Some went for cutesy gifts, and a few others gave me gifts that were actually for me – massage vouchers and bath goodies – which I gratefully accepted. My cousin Abby was giggling uncontrollably as I took her present off the pile, which I soon understood when I opened it to reveal a thick black vibrator. "Since the baby daddy isn't going to do the trick," she cackled while I dealt with the duelling emotions of wanting to murder her for my public embarrassment, and wanting to try the thing out when I got home. "Thanks, Abs," I said, rolling my eyes and carefully avoiding looking in Mum's direction as I put the box on the floor and moved on to opening some less offensive gifts.

After gifts were opened and the paper was cleared up a little, I stood up to make a speech. "Thank you all for coming," I told the group of women. "A *huge* thank you for all of these amazing gifts. I know I'll make good use out of all of them." I heard a little snort from Abby's direction, which got a few others giggling as well. I raised my voice a little, ignoring them. "And most importantly, thank you to my amazing friend Carrie for hosting this afternoon! I couldn't have done it without you." I paused for a breath as everyone applauded for Carrie. "Jack and I know how lucky we are to have this opportunity," I continued, feeling myself getting slightly teary. "There were times I thought I'd never be a mum, and even though I would have had a full and complete life anyway, thanks to all of you, this really means a lot to me. So, thank you all for coming out and showing your support today." I sat down abruptly before I completely lost it, and everyone started applauding. Mum came up and gave me a hug as the chatter in the background started up again.

"That was beautiful, baby girl," she smiled, and I hugged her a little more tightly. "I meant it," I said sincerely. "Every word. Thank you for supporting me. I know this isn't your dream for me, but it really does mean the world to me."

She smiled, her eyes shiny with tears. "Oh, dreams," she scoffed and gestured with her hands as if to shush the notion away. "Honey, you're happy, I'm happy, and I'm going to be a Grandma for the first time! I really couldn't be more thrilled."

I smiled at her, tears in my eyes. I was so appreciative for everything she said, it was hard to hold it together. I focused my attention back on the party, trying not to completely lose it.

People started to head off not long after, and I insisted on staying to help Carrie clean up, despite her protests of how I should be pregnant and putting my feet up. "I put my feet up all morning while you got the house ready," I pointed out. "That wasn't part of our deal. I'm staying!"

When the house was tidy and my car loaded up with all of the gifts I'd received, I headed home. I knew Jack was at home and making dinner for the two of us, although I wasn't particularly hungry after a day of party food. Although we hadn't come back to the names discussion, things had been pretty normal since our disagreement on the last day of school. It did concern me a little to think that perhaps the only reason things were normal between us was that we were avoiding the big issues, but I also wasn't in the mood to deal with it today. The kid would get a name sooner or later, and when the time came I'd probably have much bigger worries to deal with.

# Chapter 20

The rest of the holidays passed by in a blur, and before I knew it, the mandatory professional development days held annually before the school year commenced were upon us once more. Although I wasn't going back for the year, I wanted to keep my hours up, plus I got paid for the PD days if I attended, so I went along. It was a weird sensation to hear everyone talking about the year ahead, knowing I didn't have my own classroom to set up or lesson plans to create. It was the first time in over a decade that I wouldn't have a class to prepare for. When the PD days were over and school began in earnest, I decided to spend a few days tidying up my own home, since I was in a working mood anyway. All of the major organisation jobs were done, but I still needed to spruce it up a bit before I brought the baby home. Maybe the nesting instincts everyone talked about were more real than I had given them credit for.

Jack came home when I was cheerfully unpacking the dishwasher, singing along to Bananarama at top note. I told him in the early days of us living together that I considered it to be law that '80s music was played while I cleaned, and to his credit he had never complained about it. "You look happy," he observed, looking me up and down. "Happy for someone unpacking a dishwasher, anyway."

I laughed and paused the song, which was blaring through my wireless speaker. "I think it's pre-labour hormones," I informed him. "The nesting instinct coming to life. I've been cleaning all day."

"Great! Keep it up. I love a good nesting instinct," Jack teased. "Does it come with an urge to make dinner?"

"Alas, no cooking urges have been found to be a side effect of the nesting instinct," I told him. "Dinner is your department tonight."

"Takeaway it is!" he boomed. "So all in all I'd say we're pretty organised parents-to-be, wouldn't you?"

"Well, parents-to-be of a baby without a name," I pointed out. "I think most people lock that in at oh, say six months? We need to at least narrow it down." Having finished the dishwasher now, I heaved myself onto one of our lipstick-red kitchen stools. "Personally speaking I quite like having both Annabel and Annie to choose from, so I'd love a name we can shorten."

He nodded. "Check. And I like having a name that's easy to spell."

"True, no crazy names here. I don't want anything super-traditional and boring, though, either. What if we each write down our top five and then we go from there?"

Jack nodded. "Seems reasonable. Top five for each sex? So I have to come up with ten names?"

"Yeah, and hopefully somewhere in those ten names we can find something we agree upon. Keep in mind I maintain the right to veto any name of a little shit I've taught in the past."

After about fifteen minutes of thinking time, I put down my pen. "Okay, I'm done. You?"

"One to go," he replied absently. "Okay… and… done! Ready?"

"I'll start," I said. "Girls' names first. Lucy."

"Short, simple, to the point," he nodded. "I'm happy with that one. No long version, though? You don't want a 21$^{st}$ Century Lucille?"

"Maybe Lucinda," I offered, "but I quite like Lucy just by itself. We can always call her Luce, too. What have you got?"

"Margo."

"You've *got* to be kidding. Veto."

"Don't tell me you've taught a shitty little Margo?"

"No, Jack. I've never taught a Margo, because it's not 1950. Next."

He grumbled a little, but struck out the name Margo anyway. "The next one I have is Trixie," he said. I looked at him in surprise. It seemed a bit like a horse name, or maybe a chocolate bar, but I didn't exactly hate it. "Keep it on the list," I said, even though I couldn't really imagine it being my daughter's name. I needed to save my vetos for the Margos of the world. "My next one is Juno."

"Absolutely veto!" he said. "I hated that movie! Okay, Cassandra."

"That's cute. Keep it. Alexis?"

"Oh, I *really* like that!" he said enthusiastically. "Easy to spell, can be shortened – a few ways, actually. Okay, keep that. Jacinta."

"Eh. Ditch it," I said.

We went through our remaining girls' names but couldn't agree on any others. At least we had a few, I thought, trying to remain positive. We moved on to the boys' list.

"James," Jack offered, and I shrugged. I wasn't excited by it but I didn't hate it, either. "Connor?" I suggested, which was approved to stay on the list.

We went through our names and ended up with Harrison and Curtis on the list as well. Not an overwhelming amount of choice, but at least we had a shortlist now. "Right!" I said. "We table this until the baby actually comes, and then we make our final decision based on what it looks like."

"Deal," Jack said in a mock-formal tone, reaching over to shake my hand. I laughed and shook his in return. It was all finally feeling real!

# Chapter 21

Two days later, it became officially real. I was at home and had been feeling uncomfortable all morning, but just thought it was the newest stage in the joys of pregnancy. As the day wore on, the tightening sensation got worse. I surreptitiously timed the pain on the contraction app I'd installed on my mobile phone and saw they were coming just over five minutes apart. I looked up at Jack – it was a Saturday, so he was home, fortunately enough. "I'm not 100% sure I'm not going into labour," I said in a strangely conversational tone.

He did an almost comical double take in my direction. "Are you *serious?* Annabel!" he exclaimed. "We have to get you to a hospital!"

I laughed. "Don't overreact. *If* it's labour – and I'm not convinced yet that it is – we'll still have ages. It's not that bad yet." As if to prove I had spoken too soon, a sharper pain hit and I winced as I put my hand on my stomach.

Jack rolled his eyes. "Yeah, it doesn't look bad at all," he muttered sarcastically. "I say we get you to a hospital and find out for sure."

I entered what I considered to be a contraction into my phone, and checked the analysis which seemed just about as confused about it all as I did. It couldn't guarantee labour, but indicated I could be in the early stages. I threw my mobile at him. "You need to call them first," I ordered. "They'll tell you if we're jumping the gun or not."

Jack called and spoke to a midwife at the maternity ward, his voice at a slightly higher pitch than usual thanks to his nerves. He told them about the tightening sensation I described to him and mentioned that the pain was about five minutes apart at a time and felt like very heavy period pain, mixed with extreme back pain. He was pale when he hung up the phone. "They said to come in."

My bag was packed already, so it wasn't a particularly challenging task to get to the car and be ready to go. "I really think I'm being silly," I told him. "We're going to get to the hospital and be sent back home again."

Jack started up the engine. "Well, you know the old adage," he said. "Better to be safe than to give birth on the kitchen floor."

"That's true," I replied, breathing a little more heavily as a sharper pain hit me. "I've heard that one."

The drive to the hospital seemed to take forever, even though it was only 20 minutes away. By the time I got there I was much less convinced that I'd been overreacting. My discomfort was increasing by the minute, and I was starting to think this was the real deal. I didn't say a word, though, because I could picture Jack double-parking and flying into the emergency room like some hysterical father-to-be in an old comedy. We walked calmly into the maternity ward and I sat on one of the armchairs in the waiting room while Jack went over to the desk and dealt with the administration side of things. I hadn't let myself think too much about the actual birth, preferring to keep my head in the sand as much as possible. We'd obviously been to birthing classes and I knew the basics of what to expect, but the amount of pain and the possibility of tearing was something I had chosen not to dwell on. Now the entire nightmarish scenario ran through my head. What the hell was I doing? Was anything worth this? Still, it wasn't as if I had much of a choice now.

"I have a present for you," Jack said when I was settled in my room. "Well, it's actually from Georgia and Carrie. Georgia asked me to give it to you when the 'fun times' started." He used air quotes on my friend's comment.

"Oh, God," I laughed. Coming from those two it could be anything. "What is it?"

"I don't actually know, it's wrapped."

I grabbed for the gift and pulled the wrapping paper off greedily. Inside I found two huge packets of M&Ms and a card, which I opened to find the following message. "Congratulations, Annie! It's labour time!" it said in Carrie's cheerful script. "We can't wait to meet your little bundle of joy. We thought we'd make childbirth a little more fun with the Official Labour Eating Game (OLEG). Enjoy!"

I laughed. We'd been playing the Fallen Oaks Primary School drinking game for nearly a year now, but since I had become pregnant not long after the creation of it the girls had suggested I turn it into an eating game instead. Every time someone committed one of the offences on our list one of the girls would turn to me, mouth "shot" and mime drinking. At our next girls' night, they would take as many shots as we'd accumulated, while I would eat a mouthful of dessert for each one. It was a stroke of genius to create one for this occasion as well. I might not have been particularly hungry, but at least it would take my mind off my discomfort.

I unfolded the piece of paper that came with the card and read through the rules.

- One M&M every time you feel physical pain
- Three every time someone says something stupid
- Five every time *Jack* says something stupid
- Two every time a nurse comes into your room
- One every time you get a text asking if the baby has come yet

At the last one I looked up and frowned. "We should probably actually tell our families we're here."

"Oh! I'm on it," Jack said, grabbing his phone, and then frowning at the screen. "Just our families?"

"For now. Well, you can message Caz and George. Tell them thanks for the eating game and I'll start making good use of it now."

Jack frowned. "Are you sure that's good for the baby? Should you be having sugar right now?"

I pointed at the third dot point. "I guess that's five M&Ms," I said, reaching into the packet and throwing them in my mouth. Jack put his hands up in surrender. "Fine, I'm going to make some calls before I make things worse," he laughed. "I'll be in the hall if you need me. Just yell. I'm sure you can manage that!"

I helped myself to an additional five chocolates.

# Chapter 22

In the end, childbirth wasn't as bad as I'd feared. It was still hell on earth, but whether it was the hormones, the drugs, or just Jack's calming presence, I entered some kind of zen-like state. Carrie had mentioned in the past that she had received the advice that just when you feel like you can't possibly keep going with the labour, the baby appears, and that seemed to be the case with me. I was just starting to feel completely mentally and physically exhausted when, in the early hours of Sunday morning, our baby came into the world.

Our baby girl.

I burst into tears when they placed her on my chest, and Jack squeezed my hand and kissed my check. "Congratulations, Mama," he gasped out, sounding almost as overwhelmed as I felt. I put a hand on our daughter's back and placed my other one on Jack's cheek, squeezing him in closer to me. "Can you believe it?" I cried. He shook his head wordlessly in response.

The nurse was talking, but I wasn't taking any of it in. It was the most surreal moment of my life, but I truly felt like the luckiest woman in the world. Our baby girl was perfect.

"HAVE YOU GOT A NAME yet?" the nurse asked. Jack and I looked at each other, unsure, since we'd still only narrowed it down to our shortlist. "Alexis?" he asked, and I nodded my confirmation. "Alexis." It was perfect for her. The decision I had stressed over came so easily, in the end.

"Alexis Yates," Jack said quietly to me when the nurse had left. I looked at him in surprise – we never had come back to the surname issue. "I really don't mind," I told him, and I meant it. Seeing our baby made the whole issue seem so laughably small.

Jack shook his head. "No, she's a Yates. Trust me, you were amazing! I just stood around being useless. You deserve to have your name passed along to her."

I smiled, touched. Then inspiration hit. "We never did discuss middle names," I said, and he frowned.

"I assumed we'd go for one of our others from the shortlist. Does Alexis Lucy work? Alexis Cassandra?"

I shook my head slowly. "No. I have the perfect name. Alexis Jacqueline."

"We never even discussed Jacqueline," Jack pointed out. Then he stopped. "Oh – you mean –"

I grinned triumphantly. "She can have my surname, but she can still be named for her Daddy. Our little mini Jack."

Jack didn't cry often, but he teared up at that point. "You're amazing," he said, squeezing my hand once more and bending down to kiss me on the forehead. "We're a family, Annie. A family!"

I smiled tenderly down at our little Alexis, then up at Jack, who meant more to me than he would probably ever know. "A family," I repeated softly. It was true. Life couldn't get any better.

# Chapter 23

The balloons entered the room before my mother did. My parents walked in, tiptoeing carefully around the corner as if their presence was going to disturb our scene.

"Mum! Dad!" I exclaimed, excited to have our first visitors. "Come and meet your granddaughter."

Jack had made most of the calls, but I'd insisted on doing the one to my parents. His Mum and Dad were thrilled as well, of course, and coming to visit soon, but I really needed to hear my parents' reaction for myself. They sounded beside themselves with excitement, and had come to the hospital immediately. Mum rushed over and hugged me. Dad hung back a little, holding awkwardly on to the collection of balloons.

"This is her," Mum exclaimed, staring at Alexis. The old Annie would have made a quip – *no, actually my baby's out in the nursery. They just gave me this one as a placeholder* – but now I just smiled peacefully up at Mum. "This is her. Do you want to hold her?"

Mum held Alexis tightly, cooing over her and grabbing her tiny fist with her fingers. "She's perfect, Annie, Jack. Congratulations!" Dad said when he finally got a turn. I smiled at Jack, because it was true. She was just perfect.

"I love the name, too. Alexis Jacqueline," Mum said. "I can't wait to tell all the ladies at the craft group. Can I announce it yet?"

"For sure! Shout it from the rooftops," Jack said. "I think we want to share the news with everyone we've ever met, don't we, Annie?"

I nodded. It was true. I wanted to share my happiness with everyone.

Throughout the course of the day Julie, Jack's parents and brother, and Carrie and Georgia all came to visit. I should have been tired, but adrenaline was keeping me awake. It was amazing how quickly you adjusted to lack of sleep, I mused. Maybe my daughter's love would provide all the energy I needed.

BASICALLY, I WAS AN idiot.

It didn't take long before sleep was all I craved. I would doze off when Alexis napped during the day, but it wasn't nearly enough for me. At night I would barely be able to fall asleep for fear of being awakened. It didn't make much logical sense, but I couldn't convince my night-time brain of that. I had the obvious disadvantage of not sharing a room with Jack, and because I was breastfeeding, Lexie slept in my room. It was all I could do to keep from bursting into tears every time I heard her do likewise.

I had stayed in the hospital for two nights before they released me. At the time I was eager to get home and start my "real life" but if I had known what awaited me, I would have been campaigning to stay in longer. Alexis was sweet and beautiful, of course, but she was also draining and all-consuming.

Jack helped out a lot during the day, since he was on paternity leave, but I was so tired that he kept getting on my last nerve with the slightest misdemeanour. On my fourth day at home Mum came over and between the two of them they convinced me that they had it covered and I should go for a proper nap. I'd just finished feeding, so I saw no reason to argue. I curled up in bed and didn't emerge for over two hours. When I woke up, I was smiling. I had the house to myself, with a note on the bench from Mum saying they'd taken Lexie for a walk. I laughed out loud, amazed by the bliss a little peace and quiet could provide. I hadn't even been a mother a full week, a realisation which led to a stabbing feeling of guilt. I shouldn't be so happy to be away from my child when she was less than a week into her life! As if on cue, my breasts were filling up and becoming uncomfortable. All my conflicting emotions meant that when Mum and Jack walked through the door, with Alexis strapped to Jack's chest, I snapped. "Where have you been?" I cried, even though I knew full well.

Mum looked surprised. "We left you a note. We just took Lexie here for a walk. She's fine, sweetheart."

I sighed. "I know, I just..." I couldn't put it into words. What was I going to say? That I felt so good when I woke up that I felt bad about it? That I'd waited so long to be a mother, I should be enjoying every moment of it and not craving sleep or some time alone?

Mum nodded consolingly. "I know, baby girl," she said. "I get it." I was grateful she was there, since Jack seemed completely bewildered by my Jekyll and Hyde act. I couldn't blame him; I was confused myself. Mum led me to the couch and sat me down. "It's a rough time, but it'll get better! I thought I was going crazy when I had you. Julie was a little easier because I knew what to expect, but it's not easy."

I probably surprised both of us by leaning over and giving her a huge hug, holding on longer than I normally would. Although Mum and I had never really had friction between us, I'd always wished we had the same kind of relationship some of my friends did with their mothers. But right now, looking at my own baby girl, I felt like I understood Mum in a way I never really had before. I couldn't imagine doing this without her.

# Chapter 24

After two weeks off, it was time for Jack to go back to work. He promised he would do the bare minimum at first and be home by six each night at the latest. I knew he was doing what he could, but the day stretching before me seemed like an eternity. I had made good use of his last few days of paternity leave by making and freezing some meals for the week ahead, so I at least wouldn't have to worry about cooking. The idea of staying at home alone with Alexis every day for a year was terrifying. It shouldn't have been; I was her mother! Surely my parental instincts would make this whole thing a piece of cake? Still, the hours loomed ahead of me, and it all just felt a bit lonely. I put the TV on all the time, even though I wasn't really watching it – just having another adult voice in the house soothed me a bit. I talked to Lexie all day. I had heard it was good for their development, but right now it was all about me and maintaining my sanity. Even though I obviously wasn't getting any responses from her, I couldn't imagine sitting around all day in silence.

I craved adult company, but Mum and Dad had gone to the beach for a week and my friends were all at work. I thought about people who timed having babies with their friends or their siblings and I felt a pang of envy. It would be so amazing to have someone to talk to about all of this, someone who was going through the same thing at the same time. On a whim I googled 'mothers' groups in my area' and sent a private message to the first local group I found on Facebook. The response was quick and friendly: "Hi Annabel, it's nice to hear from you! We'd love to have you and little Alexis along to one of our meetings. Most people choose to wait until their children are a few months old before they bring them along (vaccinations etc!) but we're happy to have you any time. If you want to wait, you've got my contact details! ~ Sarah."

I mentally kicked myself. I had Alexis booked in for her six week vaccinations, but hadn't even thought about her being too young to be around other babies. I sent off a reply: "Hi Sarah, of course I'll give it a little while to make sure Lexie is all protected! I just wanted to see if I'd be able to join your group in time. It sounds great – I'll definitely get in touch when she's a little older. Thanks, Annabel." I briefly wondered if I sounded too defensive, if I'd be better to admit I just made a first-time parenting mistake, but I didn't have the mental energy to worry about it right now.

Then Alexis started crying, alerting me to her dirty nappy, and all thoughts about Mothers' group were forgotten.

IT DID GET EASIER, as Mum had promised, as I'd hoped. Mum and Dad started popping around a couple of times a week to see us or just to drop over some bread and milk to get me through the day without having to go to the shops. Georgia and Carrie vowed to leave work "at 3.06pm" once a week to come by and visit for a few hours before Jack got home. Carrie had to pick up her kids from day care on the way and bring them over, but they were no trouble: Aria cooed over the baby and even nursed her when she was allowed, while Lachlan played in my small backyard. It was amazing having some adult company for a couple of hours, especially since Jack hadn't always stuck to his promise of being home by six. Even more amazing was the fact that they usually brought food along, a takeaway cheeseburger or a slushie. Aside from the sugar and fat content providing me with an instant boost, I loved it because it reminded me of our lives before Alexis, when we'd go for an after-school snack or make time to visit a drive-thru on our way to a Professional Development session.

"I'm trying to get out during the day," I told the girls during one of their visits, "but it's really hard. It just seems so much easier to stay in. Most days I don't even get out of my pyjamas," I admitted, gesturing at the day's ensemble. "The worst part is, I feel like I should be more grateful. This is what I've always wanted, and I'm whinging about having to actually spend time with my baby." To my horror, I felt my eyes filling with tears. Ever since I fell pregnant, it hadn't taken much to get me crying. I thought it would end when the baby was born but if anything, it had worsened. Alexis was just over four weeks old now and it seemed the end of the tears was nowhere in sight.

"What you're feeling is completely normal," Carrie said firmly. "We all go through it. Isn't that right, Georgia? Your hormones are all over the place, you're not getting enough sleep and the only person you're spending your day with can't even talk back. Of course it's going to be a struggle."

"How's Jack going with it? Is he helping, or do you need me to kick his arse?" That was Georgia's contribution to the discussion.

I hiccupped out a little laugh through my tears. "He's being alright," I said slowly, "but obviously I'm doing the lion's share of the work. By the time he gets home he's tired and yeah, he'll spend some playtime with Lexie or maybe give her dinner, but all the bathing and everything's done by then. I'm the one getting up in the night. I'm at the point now where I'd happily give him my boobs if it meant I got to be the one to sleep through."

Carrie giggled. "The mental image of busty Jack is pretty funny, though."

"How long are you going to breastfeed for?" Georgia asked.

It was something I'd been giving some thought to. Carrie and my other friends with kids had all breastfed for about a year. The thought of it just about killed me. I didn't enjoy breastfeeding – yet another thing to feel guilty about! – and I didn't find it particularly easy. "I'm not sure," I said. "I guess I was aiming for a while yet, but it's not going that well. Carrie and everyone else seemed to do it for ages."

"Oh God," Georgia said breezily. "You really needed to know me when Michael was little! I breastfed for like, a minute and a half. Well, a month, anyway. I'm just not cut out for that sort of thing long-term."

I thought about this. Michael was a perfectly well-adjusted, healthy kid and until right now, I'd had no idea he hadn't been breastfed for long. Did it really make a difference in the long run? "I'll talk to Jack about it," I said. "Maybe stopping early wouldn't be the worst thing in the world."

# Chapter 25

As it turned out, at least in Jack's eyes, it was close to the worst thing in the world.

"I just don't think you've given it a fair go," he argued when I brought the idea of ceasing breast-feeding up to him later that night.

I growled in frustration and impulsively ripped my breast-feeding top to the side, revealing my red, swollen right breast. Jack winced, as if I'd shown him the most repulsive thing in the world; I had a feeling it was the breast itself, more than the mastitis, which offended his eyes so. "Does this look like I'm not trying? It's easy to say when you're not the one who's losing sleep at night or going crazy during the day just trying to get the kid to feed," I snapped.

"I'm just thinking about the baby," Jack protested.

For the record, that is the single worst thing you can say to a new mother on the brink.

I exploded.

"Oh, *I'm* not thinking about the baby? Literally *all I do* at the moment is think about the baby! You at least get to escape the house during the day," I raged.

He hit back with the inevitable response: "To *work,* Annie! I 'escape the house' to go to *work*! I'm not going to parties. I work and I come home to you and Alexis. I'm not sure what else you want from me. I can't stay home with you; that's not an option for me. I'm the one who's fucking supporting us!"

I glared hotly at him. "Yes, because I'm not contributing at all, is that right? For the record I'm still getting my maternity pay, and even if I wasn't, aren't you the one who was on his high horse while I was pregnant about how you were going to support your new family? Because that's what we are, Jack! We're a *family*, in case you'd forgotten!" My voice was getting louder by the second. On the plus side, at least I didn't feel like crying this time. The anger was propelling me through. "We might not be the family you've dreamed of, but this is the one you've got! The one you signed up to! This whole thing was your Goddamn idea in the first place, or have you forgotten?"

"You don't have to remind me. I don't have any life outside of the two of you! I go to work, I bust my balls, and I come home and I help look after Alexis. I'm not sure why that's so much easier than just staying home?"

My blood boiled and I could feel my face turning red with fury. "Yes, because I sit around watching Netflix all day, is that right? If you think this isn't work, Jack, I challenge you to come along and try it out for yourself. You wouldn't last a day!"

Alexis started crying at that point and we both looked over in surprise, as if we'd forgotten she existed. In hindsight, the only real surprise was that she'd let us rage at each other for so long before reminding us of her presence. Her tears put out the fire in us, though. I was still mad, but my only instinct then was to go to her. Jack reached for her as well, but I pushed him away. "Go shower," I said stiffly. "I'm sure you've had a hard day at work, after all."

Jack looked like he was about to answer back, but he just shook his head and left the room. I cuddled Lexie closer to me and closed my eyes, inhaling her scent. She truly was the most precious thing in the world to me, but my mind was whirring. Jack and I had never fought before we had Alexis. When was all of this going to get easier?

THE NEXT DAY, JACK apologised. "I shouldn't have said all of that. I know how hard you work," he told me. "And of course I'm not going to make you breastfeed if you're not comfortable. That's not good for you *or* the baby. I'm sorry," he finished, putting his arms out for a hug. I hesitated only momentarily before I stepped into his arms and hugged him back.

The truth was, I had already decided to stop breastfeeding. It wasn't 1920, Jack didn't own me, and he couldn't tell me what to do with my body – even if she was *our* baby. I decided to keep all of that to myself for the moment, though, and just murmured back "I'm sorry, too. I know it's not easy for you, either."

He smiled and stepped back. "So we're okay?" he asked and I nodded, even though I wasn't completely sure.

# Chapter 26

When Alexis was three months old, Carrie and Georgia booked me in for a night out. I was torn between excitement over the change of routine and a complete lack of desire to do anything that involved putting on actual clothing. I'd started to lose the baby weight, but so slowly that I was still in maternity clothes. Going to a nightclub wasn't super appealing. I told them so on one of our afternoons at my place and they laughed.

"We're in our thirties, Annie. We're not talking about clubbing," Georgia said.

"Yeah, we're just as old as you are! Well, nearly," Carrie teased. "A nice dinner, maybe a few drinks, is all we're talking about. Have you even had a drink since you got pregnant?"

I shook my head. Actually, I'd stopped drinking over a month before we started trying for a baby. Then of course I'd been breastfeeding, and after that I guess I'd just lost the taste for it. The idea of a cocktail *did* sound pretty amazing right now.

"Then it's settled! Jack can stay in and mind Lexie – sort out a date and a time with him. We'll swing by here and we can all head in together," Carrie said triumphantly.

I sorted out a night with Jack, promising him his own Saturday night on the town in return whenever he wanted. When the night came, I squeezed into a black dress I'd worn before I was pregnant. It was definitely on the fitted side, particularly now, but with some tummy-sucker undies, I thought I looked pretty decent. I curled my hair and put on a bit more make-up than usual. It was just a fairly casual night out with my two best girlfriends, but that was a special occasion for me after so many months. I knew I should have felt sad about leaving Alexis for the first time, but she was in good hands and, to be honest, I couldn't wait to just be Annabel Yates for the night, rather than Alexis' Mum. The girls exclaimed over how "hot" I looked when they pulled up, so I knew I'd done something right. Jack offered to drive us into the city to save some money on cab fare. When we arrived, I leaned over and kissed my daughter on the forehead, then kissed my fingers and stuck them on Jack's cheek from my position in the backseat. "Love you both, bye!" I yelled, leaping out of the car. The girls chimed in, calling out "love you, Jack!" I saw him shaking his head and grinning as he drove off.

We had decided to go to a fancy cocktail bar in the city where we'd been once for a work function. They had delicious but expensive tapas and fancy, fruity cocktails that made my mouth water to think about. I knew I had to pace myself – after over a year without alcohol, it wouldn't take much to get me under the table tonight! When our drinks arrived, we clinked them together and yelled "cheers!" loudly, erupting into giggles. I felt ten years younger already.

The night progressed with lots of laughter and gossip. They did most of the talking, filling me in on the latest at school. I'd always loved my job, but I really didn't miss it, I thought, feeling a sudden pang at the thought of my new life at home with Alexis. I had been so excited to get away for the night, but now that I wasn't at home with my baby, I found it was the only place I wanted to be. I quickly pushed the thoughts of her out of my mind. This was my one night to just be me, and to have fun with my friends. I wasn't going to wish it away. For the first time in nearly a year, I was going to just live in the moment.

"Anything new in your world?" Carrie asked when they'd finished telling me how our laziest co-worker had snuck home before our first aid course, citing what had to be his twelfth "family emergency" of the school year.

I shook my head. "Same old, same old. I am finally going to give that Mothers' Group a call though, and Jack and I've agreed to start taking Alexis for family walks when he gets home from work." Since our argument nearly two months earlier we'd been working hard to make things as positive as possible between us, although we never talked about the argument again. Jack had been at his work long enough to earn a little flexibility and he now worked through lunch and finished at 4 on a Wednesday, which usually got him home by 4.30. Now that I had stopped breastfeeding, we took turns at waking in the night for Lexie, who now slept five nights a week in my room and two in his. Since he was working, I figured it was only fair that I take on a few more "night shifts", but just having a couple of nights of quality sleep a week made all the difference. The walls were thick enough that I could barely hear her on Jack's nights and when I did, I was still able to roll back over and go to sleep. The extra sleep I was getting really elevated my mood, although I did feel slightly guilty about Jack having to go to work after an interrupted night. The walks were our latest idea to encourage family bonding, and I was looking forward to having a bit more of a routine and something to look forward to at the end of the day.

"My cousin Olivia wants to have a family reunion," I added, trying to think of something to contribute that didn't revolve around my baby.

"Is that the cousin who thinks you're a lesbian?" Carrie asked, and I nodded in confirmation.

"I don't know why people think you're a lesbian," Georgia said, shaking her head. "I mean, if you were a lesbian I feel like you'd be really out and proud about it."

Carrie laughed. "Yeah, and every time we paid out on you about *anything* you'd be all *stop. That's homophobic.*"

I joined in the laughter. "I totally would, too." I paused, looking wistfully out across the dance floor as I considered this. "That'd be fun."

Georgia shook her head. "Unfortunately you're stuck with us heteros, and it's no picnic, I'm afraid."

"Ain't that the truth," I said grimly. "I'm not sure if there's any talent here tonight." We looked around, trying to scope out guys who seemed available, but everyone was there in large groups so it was hard to tell.

I was on my second drink by that point and starting to feel the effects. "We should dance!" I exclaimed to my friends, who were decidedly more sober than I was and who exchanged a look that could only be described as withering. "Come on," I pleaded. "It's my first night out, after all..."

They rolled their eyes at each other, but got up anyway. There was no guilt trip like a new mother guilt trip. The bar only had a small square dance floor, but there weren't many people up there. It was just after 10pm which meant the night was just getting started for most others, although it was nearly my standard bedtime lately. The adrenaline of the night out must have been keeping me going. Of course, the long nap I'd had that afternoon while Jack took Alexis to visit his parents didn't hurt. I whirled and whooped my way around the dance floor while Carrie and Georgia moved their bodies to the music in a far less enthusiastic fashion.

At one point during my whirling and whooping, I smacked into someone standing by the bar. A male someone. A hot male someone. I hit his back, but when we both turned around, I felt something shift inside me. I'd like to say it was fate or love at first sight, but I was basically just horny. Drinking wasn't the only thing I hadn't done for over a year.

"I - I'm sorry," I stammered, recovering my composure. I flashed him a big smile – everyone had always said my smile was my best feature. Well, that and my boobs, which were looking pretty fantastic tonight in my too-tight dress. I pulled down on my hem as subtly as possible, trying to show The Girls off. "I didn't see you there. I guess I got a little overexcited."

He smiled back, showing off perfect teeth. He wasn't classically gorgeous, but he was just my type. Light brown hair, just a little stubble, and green eyes. "No worries," he said casually. "I noticed you earlier, actually. Looks like you're having a good night."

"Very good! It's my first night out since having my baby." As soon as the words were out of my mouth, I regretted them. If I'd had any chance at all with this guy, it was gone now.

"Oh! So your husband's at home minding the baby?" he asked, and I wondered if it was possible he was trying to suss me out. I went for the easiest possible explanation, given my unusual circumstances. "Single mother," I said breezily. Feeling emboldened by the alcohol, or maybe just the lust I was feeling, I added "do you dance?"

"Um..." He glanced back at his group of friends, who seemed to have gone on talking without even realising he was otherwise occupied. "It's not my favourite thing in the world. But I'd buy you a drink?"

My heart skipped a beat. "Sounds amazing!" I said, more than happy to take him up on his offer.

# Chapter 27

As it turned out, my girls' night ended up being anything but. After that I barely saw Carrie and Georgia again, aside from shooting them a quick wink as this guy – Kurt – walked me to the bar. Carrie winked back and Georgia shot me a thumbs up. I grinned back at them, knowing they wouldn't mind if I abandoned them for a while.

Kurt asked all the right questions, including the sex and name of my baby. I answered them with all the expected enthusiasm, but I didn't really want to talk about Alexis, and I was sure he wasn't really interested in hearing about her. I was hoping this night was moving in a different direction. As soon as I could, I moved the conversation to him, because we all knew I didn't have much to talk about other than Alexis at the moment! I learnt that he was in IT in the city and was out tonight celebrating a mate's birthday. He had recently broken up with his girlfriend, which I took as a warning that he wasn't up for anything serious. It was fine by me.

After another hour of talking and drinking together, he put his hand lightly on my thigh, and I felt my body respond. He moved in softly and kissed me, his tongue exploring my mouth. Our kissing became deeper as I tried not to think about how much I'd always hated public displays of affection. Carrie and Georgia had moved back to the table a long time earlier and I knew they'd be able to see us from their vantage point. I cringed inwardly and found myself pulling away from Kurt, even though every part of me wanted to keep going.

"Is everything okay?" he asked, looking a little taken aback.

"No, it's fine," I blurted out. "I just – sorry. I just don't really like doing this sort of thing in public." I paused, having an inner debate with myself before saying what I knew I would all along. "Maybe we could go back to your place?"

I'M NOT A ONE-NIGHT stand type of girl. I had never really felt the desire before, and I'd watched far too many murder mysteries to be comfortable going back to some strange guy's place. Before Adam, I'd only been with two other guys. But aside from the physical desire, I needed to feel wanted, to feel desirable. Even when I was with Adam I'd rarely felt that way, and the last person who'd seen my naked breast was a gay man who had looked like it was the most offensive sight on earth. You couldn't really blame me for being carried away by a little attention.

Of course, the lure of the physical pull couldn't be ignored, either. It was lucky that Kurt lived in an inner-city apartment only a five-minute walk from the bar, because I could barely keep my hands off him long enough to get into his building. I had shot Carrie and Georgia an apologetic look on my way out of the bar but they had waved me away, with Georgia making a vulgar thrusting gesture that I hoped Kurt didn't notice.

When we got to his apartment we headed straight past his roommate and into Kurt's room, where he pressed up against me, kissing me more urgently. I could feel him growing hard against me. He stopped kissing me and went to tug the bottom of my dress up.

I stopped suddenly, horrified. "Let me just go freshen up," I said, feeling like a dame from an old movie but unable to think of anything else to say. I grabbed my handbag and walked into the bathroom as casually as possible, where I tugged off my beige tummy control underwear. I rolled them up into as small a ball as I could manage and walked back into the bedroom, hoping I looked mysterious and sexy, rather than like someone who was carrying unflattering underwear in her bag.

"It's about time," Kurt grinned as I walked back in and threw my bag to the side. He pressed up against me again, even more aggressively this time. He reached for the bottom of my dress and pulled it up over my body, stopping to admire me. "Commando," he said approvingly, and I giggled in a way that I hoped came across as coquettish rather than embarrassed. He reached behind me and snapped open my bra. He was clearly a boob man, which was great for me since my thighs were nothing to write home about. I stripped his clothes off in return and felt myself getting even more turned on at the sight of him. God, it had been a while. I had the presence of mind to ask about a condom, which he produced. A surprise pregnancy – or worse – wasn't something I wanted to be dealing with when I had an infant at home.

Kurt virtually threw me on the bed. The sex was rougher than I was used to, but more exciting as well. I had a fleeting thought of his roommate being able to hear us, but I couldn't keep it down if I tried. I didn't want this feeling to ever end.

Afterwards Kurt collapsed on top of me, and I wrapped my hands around his back, revelling in the post-coital glow. He rolled off me almost immediately, and I grinned over at him. "I don't normally do stuff like this."

"Well, you can't tell," he laughed. "You should definitely do it more often." We lay silently beside each other in the dim light, each trying to catch our breath. The silence started out comfortably enough but grew more loaded as the minutes went on.

"I'm glad I found you at the bar," I said, and he nodded his response wordlessly. I bit my lip, suddenly unsure of myself. Since I'd never gone home with a guy on the first night before, I'd also never had to deal with what came afterwards. Should I assume I was sleeping there or just arrange to head home? I decided the safest plan was to offer to leave and see what he said.

"So, I guess I should get going?" I asked, and he nodded lazily.

"Yeah, sure. I can call you a cab," he offered. No suggestion that I should stay, then. I felt suddenly cheap, even though I hadn't wanted anything more than a night with him. It wasn't as if I had been expecting him to beg me to stay, but some kind of a mild protest about my leaving so soon would have been appreciated.

I grabbed my bra and dress and pulled them back on, then headed into the bathroom for a toilet trip and to slip on my knickers. I might have felt cheap, but I could at least go home with my underwear on.

# Chapter 28

I slept in the next morning – unsurprising, considering the late hour I got to sleep, but I was gratified to realise my body clock would even let me sleep in after Alexis' usual early morning wake-up calls. Last night's action had truly relaxed me for the first time in months, and it had been a deep, blissful sleep. I might not have been too happy about the way my time with Kurt had ended, but that part was worth it, at least.

When I walked downstairs, still in my pyjamas, Alexis was lying on her mat on the floor and Jack was making breakfast. He typically cooked up a big breakfast on a Sunday, one of my favourite perks of living with him. I went over and gave Alexis a quick kiss, trying not to interrupt her while she was happy. "Morning!" I said cheerily to Jack. "Thank God for bacon. I'm nursing a bit of a hangover over here."

He nodded, not looking up from his cooking. "You came home pretty late last night," he said in a voice that would have seemed more casual if he wasn't deliberately avoiding my gaze.

"Yeah," I giggled, suddenly unsure of what to say. "We had a fun time."

He looked up then. "I mean, Carrie and Georgia came back here without you."

I mentally kicked myself. I'd left my friends when we were on our second drink and hadn't realised Carrie must have cut herself off then so she could still drive home from my place. "Oh, yeah," I said vaguely. "Well, I... I met someone," I said, my voice stronger now. It wasn't as if I'd done anything wrong. Jack wasn't my boyfriend. I was allowed to meet someone, for God's sake!

"Oh, right," he said flatly. It must have been what he assumed, because he didn't sound surprised, but he did sound a little pissed off.

"Problem?" I asked as mildly as possible.

He shrugged, still not meeting my eyes. "I just thought I was minding Lexie so you could have a night out with the girls, not so you could go home with some stranger. I didn't realise that was something you were looking for right now. I mean, Alexis is only a few months old."

When I replied, there was a hard edge to my voice. "I might remind you that we're not actually a couple, Jack. Am I supposed to live like a nun just because I've had a baby?"

"Well, you did live like a nun *before* you had a baby," Jack snapped.

I stared at him, feeling like I'd been slapped. He wasn't wrong, which made it even worse. My sex life had always been pretty limited, but I never thought he would throw that in my face like it was a negative thing. "Wow," I muttered.

"I didn't mean that," Jack said, instantly looking guilty. "I just thought your priorities would be somewhere else. You don't see me out trying to meet guys."

"Well, maybe you should! Go out, get laid, come home happy," I cried. "It has to be better than the way we've been lately."

There was a silence as Jack thought this over. Then he sighed. "We really haven't been great, have we?"

I shook my head sadly. "No, and we always were before. I don't get why we're at each other's throats the way we are. I suppose the sleepless nights don't help."

"Plus, it's a strange situation," Jack pointed out. "We're living like a family, but we still have our own lives. It's not often that one parent goes out and gets some action while the other one stays home and minds the baby. There's bound to be a little confusion. Besides which, I think all couples fight more after they have their first baby, anyway. Add in our circumstances and I guess it's not surprising we're arguing."

I nodded. His words made sense, and I had to admit that I hadn't been seeing things from his point of view the night before. I might have told Jack to go out and get some action, but how would I really feel if he went home with some stranger while I stayed at home alone nursing a crying baby?

"You're right," I told him. "It's been a crazy time, but it always is when new parents are involved. Things will get better."

*They have to,* I added silently.

# Chapter 29

When the phone lit up with Georgia's name later that day, I assumed she was ringing to hear all the gossip about the night before.

"Hey, babe!" I exclaimed into the phone. I was surprised to be greeted by silence. "Georgia? Are you there?"

Another moment's silence, but this time I heard her sharp intake of breath on the other end. "Annie, are you free to talk?" she asked, and I realised she was choking back tears.

I held one finger up to Jack, who was nursing Alexis on the couch beside me, and went into the next room to talk in privacy. "What's up?" I asked when the door was closed behind me.

I knew what she was going to say before she said it. Of course, there was only one thing her call could be about. "It's Mum," she cried. "She has a really bad fever and she's been rushed to the hospital."

"Oh, Georgia." I closed my eyes. Georgia's mum had been doing so well in her battle with cancer that we'd all started to take a breath. We'd stopped asking her for regular updates about her mum's condition, so confident were we that she was doing okay. Georgia had even started making little jokes about it, although I knew that was her way of coping with the unthinkable. "I'm so sorry. What are they saying?"

"They said she'll need to stay in to make sure it doesn't lead to something more complicated. Ugh, Annie, I just... I just feel like shit. I really thought she was doing okay. It's like I can never just relax about this."

I nodded, even though she couldn't see me. I hadn't known much about the illness before Georgia's mother was diagnosed, having been thankfully untouched by it in my own family, but I knew enough to understand that something as seemingly straightforward as a fever could be life-threatening for cancer patients. "Are you at the hospital?" I asked.

"No, I'm at home. Michael's got a cold and I didn't want to risk giving her anything if I've caught the bug as well." She began crying in earnest. "I just want to give my Mum a hug."

"Want a visitor?"

"No, I'm okay. I just wanted to talk. Mike's keeping me company," she said. "I'm in good hands."

"Okay. I'm so sorry," I said again. "Please let me know if you need anything, okay? Even if it's just an ice cream or something."

"You know you can always count on me to ask for ice cream," she said, laughing through her tears. "I'll let you know."

We hung up and I paused to compose myself before I went out to the living room again. Georgia's line – *I just want to give my Mum a hug* – repeated in my head on a loop. It was such a simple, sad sentiment.

I went back out into the living room, where Jack was sitting on the couch with our baby. I gently rubbed Jack's back, then impulsively bent down and gave him a kiss on the cheek. Without a word I grabbed Alexis out of his arms and held onto her tightly. Jack looked at me quizzically. "Is everything okay?"

I smiled sadly as I looked down at my daughter. I would fill Jack in on everything later. For now, I simply said "just counting my blessings."

# Chapter 30

A fortnight later, Jack took me up on my offer of a Saturday night out so he could have a night on the town with some of his guy friends. I was worn out and it suited me completely to put my pyjamas on and order pizza, so I didn't think much of it as I said goodbye to him and settled in on the couch. I had put Alexis to bed already and could see from the monitor that she was out like a light. My toughest choice was what to watch on TV. All in all, it was a pretty good night in.

I'd been watching mindless TV for a couple of hours when my phone flashed up with a message from Georgia in our three-way chat. I checked it nervously, but it was just a photo of her son dressed in a red wig that Georgia's mum had purchased when she was undergoing chemo, before deciding she preferred to wear turbans and scarves. Michael was pouting, hamming it up for the camera. The picture made me smile. Mike was normally much more reserved, like most teenaged boys, and I knew he was doing it to cheer his mother up. "LOL!" I wrote back. "Great look for Mike!"

Georgia's mum had ended up staying in the hospital for on-ly a few nights, but she was far from out of the woods. Her medical team had discovered that the cancer had spread, and the long-term prognosis wasn't great. Georgia wasn't coping very well, naturally enough, but Carrie, Michael and I all tried our best to keep her as cheerful as possible. Ryan, to his credit, was also dealing pretty well with the whole situation. He had not yet got to the stage of meeting Georgia's parents, but he was a great distraction for Georgia and was, she said, a pretty great listener. I was pleased she had him.

My phone dinged again, this time with a message from Carrie replying about the picture of Michael.

**Carrie:** He should wear that everywhere.

**Carrie:** By the way, I've been thinking. Our group chat needs a name. All good group chats have names.

I smiled at the obvious attempt to keep the conversation light, then replied.

**Annie:** Bob.

**Carrie:** Lol. I'm serious!! The Three Musketeers?

**Georgia:** Because we're 94 years old. The Trio??

**Annie:** So unimaginative. Huey, Dewey and Louie?

**Carrie:** The Threesome.

**Annie:** I am absolutely NOT contributing to a group chat named "The Threesome"! Imagine if someone came across our phones! I got in enough trouble from Jack for picking up a guy. He'll think I'm into super kinky shit if he sees THAT.

**Georgia:** My son would probably find it and be too embarrassed to ever mention it! Haha.

**Notification:** Carrie has renamed your group 'The Threesome'.

**Annie:** Carrie! Noooo! You pervert!

**Georgia:** It's always the quiet ones...

**Georgia:** Plus, now I'll have social services knocking on my door.

**Annie:** Because they really care about that sort of thing.

**Carrie:** Like YOU'VE never had a threesome, George!

I was still giggling to myself and replying to messages when Jack opened the front door. "Hey," he said softly. "Alexis asleep?"

I nodded, pointing at the monitor. "You don't need to whisper, she's out like a light. How was guys' night?"

He came and settled on the couch beside me. "Well, actually... I kind of used that term loosely. It wasn't really a guys' night. Well, I guess it was, depending on how you look at it. I... I actually had a date."

I frowned, his words taking a moment to sink in. When they did, I got a sick feeling in the pit of my stomach. I tried to look more casual than I felt. "You did? Why didn't you tell me before?"

He hesitated. "It was actually my second date with this guy. We met up for coffee last week during my lunch break. I guess I wasn't sure how you'd react and I didn't want to say anything before I knew what it was."

To be honest, I wasn't thrilled. It was stupid, but I'd always felt slightly envious when Jack met someone new. It was nothing to do with wanting him for myself, or whatever people might assume if they heard that. Having a close friend meet someone was always going to be a little difficult, since most of the time the nature of your friendship changed as a result. Things had always been so good with Jack, it was only natural not to want them to change.

This, though, was something completely new. I didn't just feel a twinge of envy like I usually did. As overdramatic as it may sound, I felt like my entire world might crumble at any minute. This was the first person Jack had met since we'd had Alexis, and honestly, it was a little devastating.

"So who is this Mr Wonderful?" I asked, unsure what else to say.

Jack grinned. "His name is Nathan and he's a doctor. The first date went well, but tonight I really felt something. I think this could be something real, Annie."

A million thoughts went through my mind. There were so many different responses I could have said. What came out of my mouth was "well, this is all really great timing for us, isn't it?"

Jack's smile faded as quickly as it had come to him. "I hoped you would be happy for me."

I sighed. "I'm conflicted. I mean, for starters you lied to me about where you were – twice – which is obviously not fun for me. Plus, what does this mean for Alexis?" *What does this mean for me?* asked a voice in my head that I tried to dismiss. "We're a family here, and now this 'Dr Nathan' comes waltzing in to take you away from us?" I hated myself for being such a bitch, aware I was starting to sound like the stereotypical nagging wife. But I couldn't stop myself.

Jack shook his head. "We discussed this before you even got pregnant. We both knew there was a chance one of us would meet someone. Hell, you already met someone, or don't you remember? Don't you think you're being slightly hypocritical?"

"That was a one-night stand!" I shot back.

Jack laughed incredulously. "So that makes it *better*? I should be sleeping around instead of actually making a connection with someone?"

"That's not what I meant," I groaned. "I just... the thing with Kurt didn't *mean* anything, and you still got shitty over that. This could be an actual relationship. You'd be upset if the situation was reversed." There wasn't much he could say to that. He'd shown through my fling with Kurt that that was entirely true. And he was right, I was being hypocritical, but he was too. It was human nature.

There was a heavy silence as we both looked at each other. It was Jack who broke it, eventually. "I get that this is hard for you, I do. But Annie... you can't expect me never to meet anyone ever again. Just like I can't expect that from you. We knew this might happen. There are no guarantees for anyone – even married couples get divorced and find new partners! It's unrealistic to think that we'll live in a bubble together forever."

I nodded silently, thinking *but I want the bubble.* It might have been unfair, but it was true. I wanted to just be the three of us for as long as possible. It was simple. It was straightforward. It worked. It was *right.* Alexis was only a few months old and already grim reality was slapping me in the face. Yes, we'd prepared for this, but talking about it and it actually happening were two different things.

I didn't voice any of that, though. I smiled up at him. "You're right," I said, because he was. It might not have made me happy, but I couldn't argue with his words. "You have every right to meet someone. I'll be fine. We'll be fine! Everything will be okay," I said, as if repeating myself would make it so.

Jack beamed back at me. "I'm relieved to hear it," he said, his voice thick. Then he looked at the muted television, clearly in an attempt to lighten the mood. "It's not too late yet. Corny sitcom time?"

"Always!"

He grabbed the remote and we settled in to enjoy the rest of the night on the couch. In moments like this, it felt just like old times. I felt like maybe everything would be alright, after all.

# Chapter 31

Three weeks later, I got to meet Jack's new man for myself. Jack had told Nathan about Alexis and me on the first date, and Jack said that although Nathan had been a bit shocked at first, he handled it all pretty coolly. I still had my head in the sand about the whole situation, but when Jack suggested Nathan come over and meet the two of us, I couldn't argue. Jack had already spent a few nights over at Nathan's place and I missed having him around. He was apologetic about leaving Alexis and me, but I knew the thrill of an early relationship and I didn't want to deny Jack that. At least if Nathan started coming over here more often, Alexis and I would both see more of Jack. Besides, I had to meet him sooner or later. I just really hoped I would like him.

I was still rushing around getting the house ready when the doorbell rang. Jack's face instantly broke into a huge grin, which pained me slightly in a way I didn't want to explore. "This'll be him," he exclaimed unnecessarily, going over to the door. I hadn't even seen a picture of Nathan before, but the tall, good-looking blond guy at the door was exactly what I would have expected for Jack.

Jack greeted Nathan slightly awkwardly – he's never been one for showing affection in front of people, even when he's in a serious relationship – and brought him inside. "This is Annabel," he said formally. "Annabel, this is Nathan."

"Hi, Nathan," I said with what I hoped was a warm smile. "It's lovely to meet you." I reached out to shake his hand, supporting Alexis with the other arm.

"And you," he replied. "I suppose if we don't get along, I get the boot."

I laughed nervously, wondering inwardly if that was true. Although Nathan obviously intended the comment to be light, it led to a slightly awkward silence afterwards. "And this is Alexis!" Jack finally added, gesturing towards the baby in my arms. Nathan laughed. "Yes, so I assumed. I've never dated a man with a baby before," he said.

If Jack picked up on the hesitation in his voice, he didn't let on. "It's a whole new world," he said, gazing at our daughter with pure love in his eyes. "She's amazing. I'd definitely recommend parenthood to anyone."

Once again, I was reminded of how lucky I was. He was right. Although we'd had our ups and downs since Lexie came into the picture – and sometimes it seemed like it was many more downs than ups – I wouldn't trade our baby for anything. Suddenly, my concerns about Jack's relationship with Nathan seemed inconsequential. This bond we had was irreplaceable.

The rest of the afternoon passed peacefully enough. Nathan warmed up and we were soon making polite, even friendly conversation. I still couldn't shake a slight, niggling feeling that Nathan wasn't the one for Jack, though. I couldn't put my finger on it, but something didn't seem right with the two of them together. At first I was concerned that it might have been jealousy, but eventually it hit me: Nathan had barely acknowledged Alexis. He didn't ask any questions about her or even really look her way throughout the afternoon. When Jack offered for him to hold her Nathan waved him away, saying "she looks so comfortable there, I'd hate to ruin it." Jack didn't seem at all put off by Nathan's attitude, but I was. I would have felt intruded on if he was all over our baby, but he could have at least shown a passing interest in her. After all, if things progressed well between Jack and Nathan he could eventually become her stepfather.

I didn't express any of this to Jack, though. When Nathan had left, he turned to me, smiling excitedly. "What did you think?" he demanded to know, practically before Nathan's car had left our driveway.

I hesitated. I could see how much it meant to him that we got along, and Jack and I hadn't exactly been in the best place lately. This probably wasn't the time or place for unreserved honesty. "He's really lovely," I said simply, and Jack beamed. "I knew you'd like him," he exclaimed. I had said very little about his new man, but my simple praise seemed to satisfy Jack, which showed how much he wanted to believe it. I knew I had made the right choice in saying nothing.

WHEN I WAS 8 OR 9, my Mum bought me a diary for Christmas. It was all pretty soft pastel colours, with pages that smelled vaguely perfumed, and most importantly, it was lockable. I loved it instantly, loved the idea of writing things in there that Julie couldn't read. Even at that age, I was an eager writer. I filled the diary each day between Christmas and New Year's Eve, thrilled to write down every mundane detail about my life, to make my small life events seem like grand adventures.

My cousin Patrick had promised me a Super Mario badge on New Year's Eve – it was his old one that he didn't want anymore, and I'd always loved it, so he said "I'll give it to you the next time I see you", which just so happened to be New Year's Eve. When I wrote in my diary about it the next day, I thought how cool it would be to get New Year's Eve gifts every year. The next thing I knew I was writing "my cousin gave me a badge as a New Year's Eve present", deliberately designed to make it sound like New Year's Eve presents were some kind of family tradition. They weren't, of course, for me or for anyone else I knew, but in my head, maybe I would read back over the entry in two or five years' time and remember it the way I had written it. I never did, always remembering instead the misguided glee I had in trying to deceive my future self.

The point of all of this?

Maybe a small part of me has never really stopped trying to deceive myself. Maybe, to some degree, we all do.

# Chapter 32

A couple of days after I met Nathan, a message flashed up in our awkwardly named 'Threesome' chat from Georgia: "Are you guys free? I'm single again ☹ Want to talk".

Surprised, I grabbed my phone. I had thought Georgia and Ryan might be something long-term, or at least that they would last longer than this. I quickly typed a reply with my one spare hand while I fed Alexis with the other. "I'm so sorry! Are you okay? Want to meet up?" It was the first Tuesday of the June school holidays so Jack wasn't home, but I knew Carrie and Georgia wouldn't mind if I brought the baby along with me.

"If you can," she wrote back. "Grindtime? Carrie, are you free?"

It took a few minutes for Carrie's reply to come in. "Omg, just read this. I'm sorry too! I'll be there. One hour?"

Although we all joked that it sounded like a gay bar, Grindtime was actually the name of a coffee shop near school. It was our usual after-school hangout, but the three of us all lived close enough to work to make it a standard meeting place during the holidays as well. I bundled Alexis up, slipping on her warmest coat. It wasn't freezing, but even Brisbane in winter gets cold, especially for a little one. I tied her tiny amount of hair up into a ponytail and set out to meet the others at Grind-time.

Georgia smiled when she saw us coming and held out her hands, indicating she wanted to hold the baby. I handed Alexis over and gave my friend's shoulder a little squeeze. "Are you okay?"

She shrugged. "As okay as can be expected. I'll tell you all about it, but I'll wait 'til Carrie's here, so you don't have to sit through the story twice." I suspected it might be painful to talk about, so I carried on with idle chatter while we waited for our friend.

Carrie rushed in a few minutes later, looking harried. "Sorry, sorry. I couldn't find any clean clothes! Too many PJ days, I guess. I'm not used to dressing myself anymore."

"No kids today?" I asked, and she shook her head. "Day care day." During the school year Carrie's mum looked after the kids two days a week and they went to care the remaining three days. Although her mum got a break during holidays, she kept her day care days for some 'me time', because she would have to pay for them anyway. Aria would be starting Prep next year, meaning Carrie's child-free holidays would soon be a thing of the past, with only Lachlan still attending day care. I would miss being able to hang out without Aria, but then again, it would be a while until I had child-free days again myself.

"So what's up?" I asked Georgia when we had ordered cake and hot chocolates. "Are you okay?"

She tried to smile. "Things had been weird for a while, but I didn't want to say anything. I guess I felt like it would make it all feel more real if I talked about it. There was nothing really wrong, it just didn't feel the same between us. So last night we went out to dinner and I noticed him checking the waitress out. She was like twenty, with this amazing rack. I said 'looking to rob the cradle?' He just looked at me and said 'you can talk!'"

"Ouch," Carrie muttered. From all accounts Georgia's age hadn't been an issue for Ryan in the past, but we both knew the comment had to hurt.

"It was just a stupid little comment, but I reacted badly," she sighed. "I told him if going out with an older woman was so bad, maybe he shouldn't do it anymore. I didn't mean it, I guess I was just looking for him to reassure me. He didn't. He said the only person who had a problem with the age gap was me."

I wasn't sure quite what to say. To be honest, from what Georgia had told me – and from what I'd seen for myself the few times we'd met Ryan – it seemed like he might have a point. Georgia was fixated on the age gap more than she probably should have been. He looked at her like he was the luckiest man on earth, and didn't seem remotely fazed by the fact that she was a few years older. Ryan's youth had been part of what had drawn Georgia to him in the first place, but it seemed to be causing some self-esteem issues for her the longer they stayed together.

"Anyway, it all went from there. We argued, and eventually I asked why we were even bothering. I mean, he wants kids! I don't want any more kids! I even thought maybe it was something I'd consider for his sake, but that's not a good enough reason." She sighed. "I guess we always had an expiration date, I just didn't want to face it. I was having so much fun with him."

"Do you think there could still be some hope there?" Carrie ventured. "It doesn't sound like either of you really *wanted* to end it." I agreed; it seemed more like Georgia had pushed Ryan away than him wanting to leave.

Georgia shook her head sadly. "Look, maybe we could make it work but long-term, I don't think it's right for either of us. He deserves to find someone who wants to get married and pop out babies. You know I'm not too sure about marriage, and my baby-making days are behind me!" I understood – having a baby of my own now, the idea of starting again when my child was 15 was unimaginable. "Besides..." she hesitated now. "I don't know how much longer my Mum has left. I want her to meet my lifetime partner, not some fling."

A silence fell over the three of us as we considered her point. Georgia's mother was home again from hospital, but she was far from out of the woods. Realistically, we all knew it was only a matter of time. She would be lucky to make Christmas with the way the cancer was attacking her body. My friend's thought process made a lot of sense and I nodded slowly. "It sucks though, doesn't it? Adulthood. Making all these rational and mature decisions," I said.

She grinned at that, as I'd hoped she would. "Hey now. I might have made one sensible choice, but that doesn't mean I'm becoming a staid old grown-up. I can still do a few men on my quest for Prince Charming."

We laughed. "It sounds like a good solution to me!" Carrie said. Although she wouldn't have a clue what to do with a man other than John, the only man she'd ever been with, she was always eager to hear about our dating lives and to live vicariously through us. Georgia's love life provided significantly more tantalising gossip than mine, though, I thought ruefully. I'd been on one date since Kurt and the chemistry had been basically non-existent. I hadn't really tried since. I was still signed up to a dating site, but I rarely logged on and never made any efforts to approach guys on there. I was too busy and far too tired.

Suddenly, Alexis broke out into loud sobs for no apparent reason. Georgia laughed as she jiggled her up and down. "My magic touch," she quipped. "Here, take her back. This is why I'm not doing it all over again."

"My poor child!" I said, taking her. "You're turning women off childbearing left, right and centre!"

"Don't get me wrong, she's beautiful," Georgia replied. "But it's also beautiful not having one around 24/7."

I dished out some stewed apple and presented it to my daughter, who swallowed it fairly unenthusiastically. "So what's new in your life?" Georgia asked, obviously ready to move on from discussing Ryan.

"Loving holidays," Carrie said through a mouthful of cake. "I never want to go back. Thinking of playing the lotto." It was a similar kind of response to the one we usually came up with when asked about our holidays.

"Don't even mention going back. I'm halfway through my maternity leave now," I said mournfully. "I'll have to talk to Ann-Marie soon about what I want to do next year."

"What *do* you want to do next year?" asked Georgia.

"I *want* to stay home, but I really need to go back, at least part-time. I've never been a big fan of the idea of job sharing, though, so I guess full-time it is. I'm too much of a control freak to share my class with someone." To be honest, as much as I wanted to stay home with Alexis forever, a part of me was ready to have my own class again. It just didn't feel like something you could admit to out loud. Most people seemed to want to stay away from work as long as possible, so I couldn't help but feel like there was something wrong with me for being eager to get back to the day job. "I'm thinking of asking for an older grade next year, maybe Year 5 or something. I'm ready for a change."

"Yes, because your life certainly hasn't had enough changes lately!" Carrie teased. "Speaking of which, what's happening with Jack?"

I grimaced. "He's spending more time over at Nathan's place. I've told him to bring him over to ours more often, but I think it makes him uncomfortable." It made me uncomfortable, too, to tell the truth. Nathan was a decent enough guy, but I still hadn't warmed to him as I'd hoped I would. I felt awkward sitting around watching TV with the two of them, but it was even worse when they disappeared into Jack's room at the end of the night, with me sitting alone on the couch. It just wasn't ideal all around. "It means I'm doing more for Lexie, obviously, which is making me tireder again. It's not a great situation, but what can you do? We all knew this might happen."

"What's the long-term plan?" Carrie asked. "If they actually last, is he going to move in with you guys?"

"We haven't got that far into it. I don't know what will happen. This is on the down-low obviously, but I'm hoping it'll be a moot point. Nathan's never dated a man with kids before, and I don't think he's loving it. He never wants to hold her or anything."

"That doesn't sound good," Carrie murmured, and Georgia nodded her agreement.

"Anyway, my current thoughts on the matter are not to worry about it and just to see what happens," I finished up. It was easier said than done, but it seemed like the only logical solution right now.

# Chapter 33

I went home thinking about Georgia's love life. I hadn't really expected Ryan to be her lifelong partner, although maybe that was because I'd only met the guy a couple of times, but I was still surprised it had ended as abruptly as it did. Love really did suck sometimes.

As if on cue, my phone dinged and flashed with a notification from Cupid's Arrow, the dating site I had most recently signed up to. I hadn't been on there long, nor had I made much of an effort with it, but apparently a user named Dan79 wanted to get to know me. I opened his message with the usual mix of hope and low expectations.

"Hey there, SunshineGirl!" he said, using the name I'd selected for myself on a whim. I didn't love the name – it made me sound like a bouncy blonde, when I was far from perky at the best of times, least of all when I had a relative newborn at home – but I wasn't going to go changing it now. Besides, "TiredandGrumpy" probably wouldn't bring the men in in droves. "I love your smile and would like to get to know you better. What do you think?"

I opened up his profile, looking first at his picture. I didn't think of myself as shallow, but I needed to at least get a mental image of the guy before delving too far into his profile. He looked like a nice guy, a bit on the larger side which suited me fine. I read through the information and smiled. He actually sounded pretty promising, describing himself as a family man who doted on his nieces and nephews. That was a good sign for Alexis. My profile listed that I had a child who lived with me, and I was glad to have that information out of the way before men contacted me. It was one less awkward conversation to have.

I had enough tokens to reply to him, so I wrote a quick message back. "Hey Dan (guessing that's your name!) I'm Annie. It's nice to hear from you! How's work going? It must be challenging to be an engineer. I'm a teacher, but on leave at the moment. I kind of miss it, but then it's easy to say that now! Hope to hear from you soon. Annie."

I quickly checked over my message again before hitting the send button. I had deliberately kept talk of my leave vague; even though he knew I had a daughter, I wasn't sure he needed to know that I was still on maternity leave!

I snuggled down on the couch with Lexie and grabbed one of her picture books, the type with thick cardboard pages and different textures on every page. I moved her fingers over the textures as I read, but they were probably more entertaining for me than for her at this stage. I read the story out loud to her, using silly voices for parts of it to make her smile.

By the time I'd finished the story, my phone lit up again. I grabbed it and read it aloud to Lexie as well in the same silly voice, making her giggle and trying not to wonder whether reading my child Internet dating messages from unknown men made me a terrible mother.

"'Hi, Annie,'" I read to her. "'I'm a little jealous of your leave. I love my work, but I'd love some time off, too! Engineering is a tough gig, yeah, but I really enjoy it. Every day is a little bit different – much like teaching, I'd imagine! What grade do you teach, when you're not on leave that is?'" I made my voice go up higher still at the end of the sentence, and Alexis giggled.

"Well, let's write back to the nice man, shall we?" I asked her, again drafting my message aloud. "'I taught Year 2 last year, but I've also taught Year 1 in the past. Hoping to go a little bit older next year when I go back. How's your day going? Busy one at work?'" I assumed not, given he was messaging me back so quickly, but maybe he was on a lunch break.

"Not too bad today," came his response after more than a half-hour pause. I'd had guys just stop talking suddenly in the middle of a conversation before, so until the phone beeped, I hadn't been sure whether I should give up hope completely. "I know we haven't been talking long, but I like the sound of you. Interested in catching up for dinner or a drink sometime soon?"

I smiled to myself. My general rule of Internet dating was to try to set up a date within the first week of a conversation; any longer than that and the conversation usually fizzled before we even met. This was a little on the fast side, but that suited me pretty well, considering I didn't have much spare time. "That would be great! Where and when?" I replied. We soon had a date set up for a restaurant at Southbank on Friday night. I messaged Jack and asked if he could do kid duty on Friday, making sure to tell him I could always line Mum up to babysit if he couldn't. Things were still slightly strained and after the awkwardness with him dating Nathan, I wasn't sure how he'd react to me going out with a new guy. When Jack wrote back saying he was free, I decided to take the opportunity to reply with "thanks. Have a date!" Better to let him get used to the idea before he came home and saw me. After a few minutes he replied saying "great. Good luck!"

I scooped Lexie up and disappeared with her into my bedroom. It was never too early to pick a date outfit.

# Chapter 34

"Same outfit again?" Jack asked, looking up at me on Friday night.

I was momentarily confused, then realised what he meant. I was wearing the same figure-hugging dress I'd worn the night I went out with the girls. The night I met Kurt. "It's not like that this time," I said tartly, fully aware of the subtext behind his statement. "But, yes. Same dress. So gay of you to notice."

He rolled his eyes, ignoring my comment. "So how do you feel about this guy?" he asked, the first time he'd mentioned my date aside from his brief text the other day.

"I haven't even met him yet."

"No, I mean, any gut instincts? You normally have a pretty good idea of whether something's going to lead somewhere when you're going in."

I laughed sardonically. "Yeah, I thought Adam was a keeper, so clearly I have a sixth sense." I didn't remind him that I'd also fallen hard for the homosexual man in front of me. "Actually, I don't really feel much either way yet." I hadn't thought about it before, but it was the truth. Normally I did have a feeling, for better or for worse, before going into a date, but this time I just felt calm about it. "Whatever will be will be."

He nodded. "Good attitude," he said, turning his attention back to his iPad.

"I know. I'm like a wise old sage. And you're alright with the baby?"

"What would you do if I said no at this stage?" Jack laughed. "Yes, we're fine. You'd better get going or you'll miss your Prince Charming."

I smiled, grabbed my bag and went over and kissed Alexis, squeezing her cheeks as I loved to do. I wondered how old she would be when she no longer let me get away with doing that. "Have a good night," I told Jack, disappearing out the door.

I recognised Dan immediately on arriving at dinner; he looked just like his photo, which was not always the case when it came to Internet dating. He didn't look in any way disappointed to see me, either, which I thought was a good sign. Since having Lexie, I had changed my profile pictures to show my full body, rather than the flattering face-only shots I'd had before. I didn't have enough time to waste by going out with guys who were scared off by a few extra kilos. It had led to a slight reduction in the amount of messages I got, but I figured the worthwhile ones would still come through.

"Dan!" I said as I approached him, and we engaged in the usual awkward dance of the first date, with me putting my hand out to shake just as he leaned in for a hug. "It's nice to meet you," he smiled, revealing gorgeous white teeth.

We headed into the restaurant and by the time our entrees came I knew that he was a "closet geek" who loved sci-fi and comic book movies; that he had six nieces and nephews; that he'd never been much of one for organised sport but he'd recently taken up basketball with some workmates and was loving it. In turn, I told him about my love of reading, my hatred for cleaning, and some funny anecdotes from kids in my previous classes. The only thing I didn't mention was Alexis. Although he knew about her existence, I didn't want to scare him off before our bread came.

It was Dan who brought her up. "Your profile said you have a child?" he asked, his tone carefully light. I appreciated the fact that he was broaching the subject.

"Yes! A daughter. Her name's Alexis," I said. "Is that cool with you?" – as if I had an alternative situation prepared if he said *no, actually, I'd rather she not exist.*

"Oh, for sure! I love kids. I hope to have a few of my own someday," he said enthusiastically. "How old is Alexis?"

"Um, nearly five months," I said.

He looked a bit shocked, as I'd expected, but recovered quickly. "Wow! Younger than I thought. So you and the father weren't together for too long after the birth, I'm guessing?"

I laughed awkwardly. This was the part of the conversation I wasn't so sure about. "Actually, we were never together. My friend Jack is the dad, but... he's gay. We decided we both wanted a child, so... Well, this was the easiest way of going about it, I guess."

There was a loaded silence as he took in the information. There were so many unconventional family situations around nowadays that ours shouldn't be so unusual, but it still always seemed to get a reaction from people. Not to mention, Dan was the first date I'd mentioned the situation to. I'd skirted around the topic with Kurt and the one other date I'd had since had barely had enough of a spark for me to even want to mention Alexis. It was a good sign that I actually wanted to share this information with Dan, but I wasn't sure how he'd react.

"Wow," he said again. "That's cool, I guess. No scary ex." He laughed awkwardly. "So, do you and the dad live together, or is it a shared custody thing?"

"No, we live together. It's all getting really interesting now though, because he's started seeing somebody." Apparently I just couldn't shut up tonight. Dan was going to run a mile from my crazy domestic situation, and I couldn't blame him if he did. There were times when I wanted to run a mile myself.

To Dan's credit he looked more interested than surprised, although that could be because he'd decided I was a better source of entertainment than romance. "Really? How long's that been going on?"

I quickly filled him in on the new relationship between Jack and Nathan, careful not to mention my uncertain opinion of the new guy. Aside from not wanting things to seem even more complicated, it somehow seemed like a betrayal of Jack to air our dirty laundry in public. "It's funny, though," I added, "Jack hadn't had much luck romantically for years before we had Lexie. We decide to have a child and bam, he meets someone!" I didn't add out loud what I was thinking: that if things progressed with Dan, Jack and I might both end up in relationships just months after having our daughter.

The conversation moved on to lighter topics – I told him about my love of old movies, he shared stories from the trip to Thailand he'd taken last year – and the night passed quickly. After dinner we strolled back towards the carpark, then stopped at the top of the stairs and continued chatting, neither of us seemingly in any hurry to say goodbye to the other. It was only when my bladder started calling that I put my hand on his arm and said "look, I hate to cut the night short, but I probably should be getting home."

He nodded his understanding. "It was great to meet you, Annie. I hope we can do this again sometime?"

I smiled. "That sounds great," I replied honestly. "You've got my number." We'd exchanged them before we met so I had his as well, but I was hoping I wouldn't need to make first contact.

"Yeah, I'll be in touch. Get home safely," he said, pulling me in for a hug and then kissing me quickly on the cheek.

I STILL FELT LIKE I was floating on a cloud by the time I got home. Jack was lying on the couch with the TV on and his book in front of him, clearly paying more attention to his reading than his viewing. He looked up when he heard me come in. "How was the big date?"

I came over to the couch, moving his feet out of the way enough to allow me to sit down as well. "It was actually really good," I said. "Too early to tell, of course, but it seems promising." On one of the few dates I'd had since Adam the guy had finished it off by saying "I'll definitely call you" three or four times in a row, only to never contact me again, so I knew not to count my chickens before they hatched anymore. Funnily enough I'd been quite hurt by the lack of contact with some men in the past, and now I couldn't remember any of their names. I should try to keep that mentality, I thought. If I never heard from Dan again it might sting a little now, but I wouldn't even remember his name a few months from now.

Jack was far more supportive to hear about my date with Dan than my night with Kurt; possibly because I hadn't actually slept with Dan, but more likely because he realised any other reaction would be entirely hypocritical, given his relationship with Nathan. It felt like old times as I filled him in on the date, before everything became so complicated. Maybe this was the solution? If Jack and I were both in happy relationships at the same time, everything would become a lot easier. Of course, I couldn't exactly will Dan to fall in love with me, so it wasn't solely my decision. For my part, though, I knew I wanted to see him again. Judging from our first encounter, he seemed to tick all my boxes. Now I just had to wait and see if he felt the same way about me.

# Chapter 35

I only had to wait until the next day, when Dan messaged me. I smiled as I read it. *Had a great time the other night. Love to see you again if you're interested?*

"For sure!" I wrote back. My sister had always advised I wait "half an hour or more, like going swimming after you eat" before responding to a guy's invitation to a date, but I'd never been one for playing games like that. "Maybe brunch or lunch tomorrow?" Julie had also told me not to suggest a date, and to decline any date within five days of an invitation so the guy wouldn't think I was too available. Man, I was breaking all 'the rules' now, I laughed to myself. I hoped the idea of a daytime date sounded casual and fun, but actually I had planned it around my baby. It was easier to ask Jack to look after the baby during the day than expecting yet another night out. I didn't mention any of that to Dan, though. Even though he seemed fine with the idea of dating a single parent, I didn't need to slap him repeatedly in the face with the reality of the situation. Fortunately he replied enthusiastically (and without a thirty minute wait between messages), so we arranged brunch for the following day at a local coffee shop.

"Breakfast on Sunday without going home with the guy on Saturday, hey?" Jack teased. "Sounds very old-fashioned."

"Maybe we'll have afternoon delight instead," I replied. Then, seeing the look on Jack's face, I added "kidding! This one might actually be a keeper. No funny business just yet."

He shrugged. "None of my business either way," he said, a clear peace offering following his tantrum over the Kurt situation. "I hope he is a keeper, though. You deserve it."

I smiled. "Thanks, Mr Delaney," I said. "I hope so, too. Wouldn't it be amazing if we were both in happy relationships at the same time?"

Jack gave a laugh that sounded more like a snort. "I'm not sure amazing would begin to cover that," he said. "It sounds completely miraculous to me."

It was true; Jack's and my love lives had never really lined up. There was a time early on in my relationship with Adam when Jack was with Theo, but although they were together for over two years in total there was only about a six-month overlap on our two relationships. It had never been an issue before, aside from one of us maybe having more free time than the other at any given time. Now, though, it would impact our lives more greatly either way. The two of us both being coupled up at the same time could lead to a smoother relationship between us, or it could further complicate things. After all, what would we do? Move two new men in with us and Alexis? That wouldn't be an easy one for her to explain at school! *You're getting ahead of yourself,* a voice in my head cautioned, and I made a conscious effort to stop my line of thought. Sometimes a second date was just a second date, after all.

IN THE END, THE SECOND date went well – even better than the first. At the end of the date Dan kissed me, and it was amazing. I'd known we had chemistry, but this was beyond my expectations. When we broke apart, I could tell from his face that he felt it, too.

After the fourth date – dinner and a movie – he invited me back to his place. I hesitated. Julie was babysitting, since Jack had already organised to go out with Nathan, and because she was sleeping over, I had as much time as I wanted. I *wanted* to go home with him, but I didn't want to risk moving things along too fast. I was really starting to like this guy.

Sensing my hesitation, Dan said, "it's totally fine if you don't want to," and that, paradoxically, was what convinced me to go home with him.

I shot a quick message to my sister, telling her not to expect me home. She'd be fine without me, but I didn't want her to worry about where I'd got to. She responded with an eggplant emoji and a winking face, so I figured I'd be in for a grilling to-morrow.

Dan lived alone, in a modest but stylish two-bedroom house, so I didn't have to worry about disturbing a roommate this time. We didn't even worry about making it to the bed-room, in fact; when we walked in, he got me a drink, we sat down on the couch together, and that was where we stayed.

We cuddled together afterwards. The sex was great, but I think what I enjoyed most of all was the feeling of wrapping myself up in his warm body. I had missed that, and it was one void my night with Kurt hadn't managed to fill, considering how quickly he ejected me from the bedroom. Spontaneously, I nibbled on Dan's ear, and he responded by squeezing my breast, and, pretty soon, we went back for round two.

We did eventually move to the bedroom after that, where he put his arms around me until we fell asleep. It was the best night's sleep I'd had in a long time.

# Chapter 36

Fairly unsurprisingly, it didn't take long before Jack raised the suggestion of Nathan moving in. Although part of me had been waiting for it, I still felt my heart thud in my chest at the words.

I took my time before responding, but my words still came out sounding blunter than I'd hoped. "Do you think that's the best solution?" I cringed inwardly at the sound of my own voice, but at least I was being honest.

He looked a bit disappointed that I hadn't immediately jumped at the idea. "I don't know how it'll work, but we're getting a lot more serious now. I'm not saying it has to be tomorrow – we've still only been together a few months – but I'm missing out on so much time with Lexie because I'm spending time at his place, and I want some quality time with you, too, babe."

I sighed. "Look, I'm not saying no. I'm just not sure if it will work. Plus, what if things continue on with Dan? Should we just move him in, too, and have orgies every Sunday?"

Jack frowned, mock-serious. "Sundays are for rest. Orgies happen on a Tuesday."

I held up my hands in surrender, smiling as I did so. "Sorry, I forgot the Number One Orgy Rule."

"The NOOR," Jack agreed in a solemn tone. "Don't forget it again. So important."

Although it felt nice that we were finally getting to the point of responding to conflict without drama, it still didn't solve anything. "Let me think about it," I told Jack, and he nodded. "I don't need an answer straight away. And don't worry, Nathan and I haven't *seriously* talked about this yet, so no pressure! He doesn't know I've asked you."

Trying to lighten the mood again, I added "you know you've only been together two months, right? You're giving commitment-phobe men a bad name. You're acting like a lesbian couple here." I knew Jack wouldn't take offence – he was the one who told me the bad joke about lesbian couples in the first place. *What do lesbians bring on the second date? A moving van. And what do gay men bring on a second date? What second date?*

As promised, I did go away and think about it. Jack was right; he was missing more and more time with Lexie and with me because of time spent with Nathan. I knew he'd be happier with all of us living under the same roof. Of course, he could choose to make his daughter – and, yes, me – the priority and not spend so much time with his new man. Still, it was only natural to want to spend time with someone you love, especially in the exciting early stages. Wasn't I starting to want to do just that with Dan? Speaking of Dan, of course, things were still new and delicate. He had accepted my unusual home life fairly well, but I wasn't sure what he'd make of me moving another gay man into my house. True, the house was technically Jack's, so he shouldn't even really need to ask permission, but on the other hand – of course he should! We were a family, and all of our lives were going to be changed by this, not just his own.

The question I had asked Jack remained in the back of my head, too. If things did progress with Dan, then shouldn't he have the right to move in, just like Nathan? And what would that mean for Alexis? Would she grow up with four parents in the house? Of course, a lot of kids had survived worse living situations, with a lot less love and comfort. Having said that, did Nathan actually love my daughter? It seemed a pretty safe bet to suggest that he didn't. Dan hadn't even met her yet, and I wasn't in a huge hurry to make that happen. Why *was* Jack in such a hurry to move in with Nathan, anyway?

I was about to give myself whiplash playing Devil's Advocate with myself, so I stopped. What it boiled down to was this: if Nathan didn't move in with us, then sooner or later, the solution was going to be Jack moving in with Nathan. I wasn't sure if having Nathan as our roommate was the best solution, but I knew that having Jack gone wouldn't be good for any of us. In the end, I had little choice but to accept Jack's suggestion, and Nathan moved his things in within the fortnight. I still felt uneasy about it all, but I had to hope for the best.

"GOD, THAT CHILD OF yours wakes up early," Nathan groaned.

I rolled my eyes. "They tend to do that, you know."

He sighed. "I'm aware that they wake up early. I *wasn't* aware of how much sleep *I'd* end up missing."

"I guess that's what happens when you move in with some-one with a six-month-old," I said, trying to keep my tone more civil than I felt. "Instant family situation for you, hey?"

It had been three weeks since Nathan moved in and things between us were tense, to say the least. We tried to keep the relationship as polite as possible for Jack's sake, but we were far from being friends. I knew that deep down, neither of us wanted to share Jack with the other, and the result was a strained feeling that never seemed to fully go away. It didn't help that Nathan seemed woefully unprepared for life with a small child. It was fair enough to complain about the lack of sleep that we were all experiencing – it certainly hadn't been pleasant since Alexis had started waking more often – but surely he knew that would be the case before he agreed to move in?

My phone lit up then with a message from Dan. I brightened immediately. Things were still progressing pretty well, nearly two months into our relationship. Jack had even suggested we have Saturday "double date" nights, which I had teased him was laughably close to my own joking suggestion of Sunday orgies. Our first double date night was set for that evening and was likely to be a fairly tame affair, but I was looking forward to it. Jack was planning on cooking a roast and we were going to have a few wines and relax on the couch. I was looking forward to Dan and Jack spending some more time together, and I hoped that having a relaxed evening in with Nathan would bring us a bit closer as well. Most of the nights we spent together ended up with him watching TV and me reading or checking my phone, so conversation between us was basically non-existent.

Of course, there was also the not-inconsequential matter of Dan finally meeting Alexis. It was probably silly to have kept them apart for so long with Lexie still so small, since it wasn't as if she'd have trouble coping if he was to suddenly disappear on her, but my protective instincts were pretty strong and I didn't want to risk anything. I also didn't want to freak Dan out and drive him away. Knowing about a child was one thing. Actually coming face-to-face with the reality of one was completely different, as Nathan was so ably demonstrating.

I had Alexis on my arm, but I reached for the phone with my spare hand and smiled as I read my message. "Hey, beautiful! Looking forward to tonight." It was simple, but just hearing from him immediately lifted my spirits. "Me too," I wrote back cheerfully. "Can't wait to see you! xo".

My phone pinged again immediately, and I grabbed it up, expecting to see a quick reply from Dan. Instead, it was a message to Carrie and me from Georgia. "I'm at the hospital," it read. "Mum's gone."

# Chapter 37

I left Lexie with Jack and Nathan and raced straight down to the hospital to see my friend, calling Dan on the way to tell him what was happening. Carrie was out with her family, but said John would drop her off to Georgia as well. Aside from Michael, Georgia didn't have much family. Her dad was beside himself with grief so I knew it would be Georgia's role to comfort him, rather than the other way around. It was understandable, of course, but I also knew Georgia would need a soft space to rest her head and just be looked after. I came to the hospital in such a hurry that I didn't have time to bring anything with me, and I didn't think the gift shop flowers would really impress Georgia. I knew that quality time together was what she needed, although I did make a mental note to cook up some meals for her for later on down the track.

I imagined myself rushing towards Georgia and throwing my arms around her extravagantly, but as I approached my steps became more and more tentative. I felt almost shy, in a strange way. Although I had lost my grandparents a few years back, I had only had limited experience with death. Georgia was closer to her mum than I was to mine, and I couldn't bear to lose either of my parents, so I couldn't begin to imagine how my friend was feeling.

"Hey," I said softly, kneeling down beside Georgia in her uncomfortable waiting room chair. "I'm so sorry, George." I reached out and she fell into my arms, sobbing. "I knew it was going to happen," she sniffled, "but I didn't think it would be so soon."

I nodded wordlessly. Georgia's mother had one of those awful deaths that is somehow simultaneously long and arduous, and sudden and unexpected. We'd all known the end was coming for some time now, but there was no real indication it would be anytime soon. Everyone had assumed we'd get the call that it was down to the last days, but Georgia explained to me now that there had been no such notice. "It was just lucky we were all there," she said. "Mike, Dad and I were all by her side."

I smiled and reached for her hand. "That's not luck," I told her. "You guys were amazing with her. She'd have been hard pushed to find a time when she was alone." It was true – Georgia had to work, obviously, and Mike was more absent from the hospital than his mum and grandad, which was reasonable for a teenaged boy. Georgia's father had barely left her bedside, though, except reluctantly to sleep or when forced out by sympathetic hospital staff long after visiting hours had already ended. Georgia had also spent most of her spare time here when she could, although she had confided in me a while ago that she found hospitals draining. Her mum had been in and out of there for the last year, but had been a permanent resident for the last three weeks. I could see the exhaustion on Georgia's face, although a lot of that was obviously the trauma the morning had brought.

"Hey, you guys."

I turned and saw Carrie approaching us in the same cautious style I had earlier. She was holding a big, cheerful yellow balloon with a smiley face on it, which she held as she gave Georgia a long hug. When she pulled back, they were both crying. Carrie gestured to the balloon with a rueful smile. "I know it's not the most appropriate thing, but I just thought you'd have a lot of flowers already."

Georgia laughed through her tears. "It's *perfect,*" she said, and I could tell she meant it. Carrie then presented her with a giant box of chocolates, which Georgia took gratefully. She used to be quite careful about not overindulging, but with everything that had been happening lately with Ryan and her mother she had, as she put it, "given up". It seemed completely fair to me.

"I'm empty-handed," I said guiltily, "but I thought I'd make you some meals if you want?"

Georgia waved my comment away. "I just need you guys here. But yeah, your lasagne sounds good too," she said, and we all laughed. It felt good to break the tension.

We moved to a couch in a smaller, more private waiting area towards the window. It was a tight squeeze, but Georgia went in the middle and it felt like the best way to support her. "Where's your dad?" Carrie asked.

Georgia gestured numbly in the general location of the elevators. "Mike took him downstairs for a drink at the coffee shop. He needed to get away from here." Her voice broke on a sob again, and Carrie reached out and put a hand on her back while I fumbled in my bag for the small pack of tissues I'd thrown in on my way out. Georgia took it gratefully and wiped at her eyes. "I just don't know how I can cope without her," she said, her voice becoming a full wail that brought tears to my eyes as well.

The three of us sat there like that for nearly an hour, not really saying much, but being there for Georgia and cracking lame jokes whenever we could to try to make her smile. Eventually Michael and Georgia's dad returned, and we stood to hug them and offer whatever words of comfort we could. Georgia's dad smiled at us with sad eyes, thanking us for supporting Georgia. It broke my heart to think that he probably didn't have close friends to look out for him the way Georgia did. Most older men didn't seem to, at least if my dad was any indication. Georgia's dad had his only daughter and his grandson, of course, but it was going to be a lonely road for such a lovely man.

Thinking we should give the family some alone time, Carrie and I left not long after that. I dropped her back to her place, the car ride noticeably silent compared to our usual singing and chatting. "Poor Georgia," Carrie said finally, looking out the window.

"I know," I murmured. "It's awful."

"I just can't even imagine what it must feel like," Carrie added. "I call my mum about everything. Imagine suddenly not having that support in the world?"

I thought of my own mum, and then of Lexie, a chill running down my spine. I couldn't imagine losing my mum, but the thought of leaving Lexie to struggle on without me was even worse. I wondered if that was how Georgia's mum had felt when she knew the end was coming. Even though Georgia was an adult, I knew it could never be easy to leave your family behind.

When I got home, I rushed right in and grabbed Alexis out of Jack's arms with little preamble. As I held her, I started sobbing in earnest, the way I'd been wanting to all day. Lexie started to cry as well, her baby wail, and I kissed her forehead gently. Jack put his arms around me and the three of us swayed gently back and forth together.

# Chapter 38

With everything that had happened, the planned roast dinner was cancelled, but Dan still came over that night. I needed the company. I was obviously devastated for Georgia, but I was grieving the loss of her mum myself as well. We hadn't known each other all that long, but we had always got on well. I knew that a lot of the time that friends who only met in their thirties might have nothing to do with each other's parents, unlike friends who meet at school, but Georgia's mum was always involved, looking after her grandson and helping her daughter out in any way she could. I knew her, and I loved her.

Although the four of us hadn't achieved the fancier dinner we'd planned, we still all spent the evening together, with Lexie of course, watching a couple of movies in the living room and having takeaway Chinese. I noticed Nathan's jaw clench slightly when Jack laughed that soon Lexie would be old enough to understand, and our M-rated movie nights would have to become G-rated affairs. I rolled my eyes. Nathan obviously loved Jack, but whether he was really ready for the reality of living with a child remained to be seen. Everyone talked about how difficult it was having a baby, but babies were so pliable and slept so much that I didn't feel like Lexie had really disturbed our lives as much as I'd expected. Having a toddler or a 6-year-old running around, though, was going to be the real challenge. I couldn't deny a large part of me hoped that Nathan would find he wasn't up to it and would leave. I didn't ever wish any harm on Jack, but I couldn't shake the feeling that Nathan wasn't right for him. For *us*.

My misgivings aside, it was a lovely evening. The films had the desired effect of taking my mind off Georgia and her mum, and although I could have done without Nathan there, having Dan, Jack and my daughter was perfect. After polishing off a couple of bottles of wine and a full block of chocolate, we decided it was time to head to bed.

Dan reached for me as soon as I closed the bedroom door. I wasn't exactly in a sexy mood, but I did feel the need to be close to him, and I melted into his arms and into bed with him. For the first time it felt like we were really making love instead of just having sex, and I realised how much I was falling for this man.

# Chapter 39

Georgia's mother's funeral was the following week. As soon as we knew what day it was going to be, Jack offered to take time off work and come along. Although he and Georgia had always got on well, I knew he was mostly coming as a show of support for me. I really appreciated it. This was the sort of thing I had really wanted when I had pictured a life with Jack so long ago: not sex and passion so much as someone to support me through the everyday things. Between living together, having a baby together and having someone to hold my hand through the tough times, it struck me that I now had all the things I had really always wanted with him. I knew I didn't take enough time to be grateful for that. I squeezed his hand as we took our spots in the church, and he smiled down at me. "Are you okay?" he whispered. I nodded. "Thank you for being here," I whispered back.

The funeral was in equal parts devastatingly sad and charmingly funny. Georgia's mum, knowing full well the day was coming, had picked some songs and insisted on a light-hearted tone for the day. A lot of people insist on such things but it's always hard to manage, given the grief shared by the people present. Georgia and her family had done their best to accommodate her mother's wishes, though, with a variety of humorous family photos on the slideshow and talk of shared jokes in the eulogy. Georgia held herself together remarkably well as she spoke, and as I hugged her afterwards, I told her how proud her mum would have been of her efforts, and of the day itself. "It's exactly what she would have wanted," I told her honestly, and she nodded, smiling. "I think so too," she said, pulling me in for an even tighter hug.

Jack and I drove home mostly in silence, each seeming to need the time for reflection. I had always found funerals quite cathartic, and this one was no exception. When we were nearly home, I turned to Jack suddenly and said, "thank you."

"I was more than happy to come," he replied, but I shook my head. "Not just for coming today. Thank you for everything. I was thinking today how lucky I am, to have you in my life." I paused, feeling a bit choked up. Jack and I had never really spoken that seriously about feelings, and he always shut down a bit if I tried, as so many men do. "A few years ago, the thought of having the life I do now would have been unimaginable. We have a beautiful daughter, our amazing house, each other. I don't think I realised until today how important all of that is."

Jack nodded wordlessly, his eyes still fixed on the road. Then, to my surprise, he said "I was thinking the same thing. I know we've been fighting a bit lately, but there's no one else I would rather go through all of this with. Truly," he added, removing his eyes from the road long enough to smile over at me. "I love you. You know that."

I did, but it was something that had mostly gone unsaid between us, and particularly from him to me. In films and TV shows featuring a gay male-straight female relationship, the characters seem to always be expressing their love for each other, but I had never found that to be terribly realistic. Of course, the straight female lead was always stripping down and changing clothes in front of the gay man as well, which I found even more unbelievable. Maybe it was to do with my own body hang-ups, but I couldn't imagine ever casually getting down to my bra and knickers in front of Jack. I also couldn't imagine it going down that well if I tried!

"I love you too," I replied. "All of the bullshit... let's leave it behind, yeah? All that really matters is we're best friends and we love our daughter."

"Deal," he said firmly. "No more bullshit."

It all sounded so simple in theory. Of course, in real life, love goes a long way, but isn't, in fact, enough to get rid of "all the bullshit". I knew Jack and I were still going to fight, especially as Alexis got older and we had to make more and more decisions about her welfare. Eventually she would leave home, and where would that leave us? Was there any point continuing to live with someone you weren't in a relationship with, when you no longer had your daughter there to bind you? Would we end up as sad 90-year-old roommates? Or would our unconventional family always bind us?

In the end, it didn't matter. All we could do was live for the now, and I was happy. No one knew where life would take them. You could marry the love of your life and they could die tragically, or the relationship could end unexpectedly. No one had any guarantees. True, Jack and I had one more complication than the average relationship, but surely every family had their little quirks.

# Chapter 40

It was my "Threesome" group chat with the girls that first made me realise something might be wrong.

Carrie and I had been keeping the chat going pretty consistently, not wanting Georgia to be alone with her thoughts for too long. Of course, we had told her we were available for cake dates and dinners any time of the day or night, but Georgia had become uncharacteristically reserved and retreated into herself more than I'd seen her do before. I wished I could help her more, but I knew she'd reach out when she was ready. In the meantime, Carrie and I kept the constant stream of messages going with observations of our day coupled with memes and Gifs designed to make Georgia laugh.

During one such conversation Carrie complained that she was "having the worst period pain today", and suddenly it felt like the walls were caving in on me.

It seems crazy to say I hadn't noticed not getting my period, but with everything that had been happening, I'd had more than enough to think about. But as she said it, it occurred to me that I couldn't remember the last time I'd had it. Since I'd stopped breastfeeding relatively early, my period had come back sooner than I'd wanted after the pregnancy, and had been mostly regular since then, so having a seven-month-old didn't account for the missing period.

*Think, think,* I told myself urgently, abandoning the message conversation. I grabbed my phone and scrolled through the calendar, trying to remember when it had last been. I vaguely remembered having to make an emergency run to the shop for tampons one day, balancing Lexie on my arm and wishing I had been more organised, but how long ago was that? It was when Nathan had just moved in, I remembered, which made it... early August. I counted back on the calendar. Even though I didn't have an exact date for it, I knew it was more than the usual stock-standard 28 days I went between periods. It looked like it was close to five weeks.

It was a Saturday morning, so it was easy enough to leave Lexie with Jack and run down to the shops for a pregnancy test, but I sat completely still on the edge of my bed for a while. I'd say I was trying to gather my thoughts, but the truth was I was stalling. Could I actually be pregnant? How would Dan cope with this? And what about Jack, how would he feel? If I put myself in his shoes, I knew I wouldn't be thrilled. Lexie was still so young, and the thought of her having a half-sibling who had nothing to do with Jack would have to hurt him. I knew I was getting ahead of myself, but this was how I always reacted when I started to panic. I got into my own head and couldn't dig myself out of there.

It was then I heard the shower stop. Dan had stayed over the night before, as he so often did on the weekends, and my panic stations flew even more into overdrive when I heard him. I didn't know if I should tell him or try to play it cool, but I knew if he took one look at me, he'd know something was wrong. Besides, I needed to get the pregnancy test as soon as I possibly could.

Dan came out, his towel wrapped around his waist. God, he looked good. "Hey, babe, you okay?" he asked, looking over at me as he reached for his pile of clothes.

I took a deep, shaky breath before I spoke, trying to sound calmer than I felt. "I just realised something," I said, ridiculously simple words for what I was feeling.

"Oh, yeah? What did you realise?" he asked, looking concerned now. It seemed my attempt at nonchalance hadn't worked quite as well as I'd hoped.

"I'm... late." I swallowed.

Not surprisingly, Dan was clueless. "Late for what? I didn't think you had any plans for today."

"No, my period... it's late. Nearly a week late, I think." I looked down at my hands, not wanting to see the expression on his face.

There was a long pause, then "do you think you might be...?"

"I'm not sure," I whispered. "Maybe."

I brought my eyes up to meet his, and immediately regretted it. His face was shutting down in front of me. "I thought you were on the Pill," was his only verbal response.

I felt the frustration rise inside me. "I am, Dan! But you and I both know nothing's 100 percent effective. Look, there's no use in panicking yet," I said, even though I was clearly doing exactly that. "I'll go down and get a pregnancy test, and then we'll know for sure."

"I can go," he said, yanking on his jeans as if his life depended on it. "I won't be long. Any kind?"

I nodded wordlessly, and Dan walked out the door. It was the longest wait of my life.

AFTER DAN RETURNED, I took the test and we both stared at it wordlessly. I wanted to hold his hand or cuddle up to him, but it didn't feel like the gesture would have been welcome, so I didn't even try.

After what felt like an eternity, the line appeared. We waited, but a second line didn't join it. "It's negative," I eventually breathed. I had expected to feel nothing but relief, and that was definitely the main thing I was feeling, but I was surprised to realise I had some mixed emotions. I knew it was the right thing – neither of us were ready, especially not in such a new relationship – but I still felt a slight, unexpected twinge. Maybe it was just a biological tool, a deep yearning for survival of the species even when it most definitely wasn't the right thing.

"Thank God," Dan laughed. It annoyed me slightly, even though I had no right to feel that way when I'd just been silently praying for a negative result myself.

"It's not 100% definite yet," I warned him. "I should probably take another test in a day or two, if I don't get my period before then. Sometimes it's just too early to tell."

He frowned at me. "Did you *want* to be pregnant?" he asked slowly.

"Of course not," I said, forcing a laugh. "I'm just being practical. My cousin took a negative test when she was trying, and a week later she found out she actually was pregnant all along. I don't want the same thing to happen to us."

Dan was still staring at me. Eventually, in a soft, dangerous voice, he said "are you really on the Pill?"

I was silent for a moment, processing this, and then I exploded. "What?" I cried, unable to believe what I was hearing. "You think I *tricked* you? Dan! I don't believe this!"

"You're avoiding the question."

"I'm not avoiding it! I'm on the bloody Pill. I've taken it every day. And if you think I'm the kind of person who would trick someone into pregnancy when I have a bloody *infant* of my own already, then..." I shook my head, unable to go on. I knew Dan was only reacting this way because he was freaked out, but I was disgusted with him. How dare he think so little of me?

"Look, I'm going to go. We both need to calm down a bit," Dan said, reaching for the door handle.

"Fine. Go," I said, hot tears burning behind my eyes. As I watched him leave, I knew things would never be the same between us again.

# Chapter 41

I messaged the girls to fill them in on the short version of events and then went downstairs to Jack, who was sitting on Lexie's floor mat playing blocks with her. "Sleep in this morning?" he asked, then stopped when he saw my teary expression. "What's wrong?"

I sobbed as I told him about the pregnancy scare and about Dan's reaction. He hugged me, then stepped back and looked at me. "Are you upset about the baby, or about Dan?"

I thought about the question. "Honestly neither, really," I said, surprising myself with my response. "I did feel a *little* bad when I saw it was negative, but I know it's definitely the right thing. So, I guess it's mostly about Dan, but honestly? Maybe I dodged a bullet. I mean, he didn't end it or anything, but I don't think it's a great sign when his first thought was that I was lying to him. I'm not sure how we'll go on after this."

"Do you want my honest opinion?"

"Always," I said with a small laugh.

"I think maybe this happened for a reason. Maybe this was what you needed to see from him, before things got more serious."

I nodded. Part of me thought it was wrong to hold something said in a moment of panic against him forever, but at the same time, didn't people say that your actions in times of a crisis revealed your true colours? This was the first time Dan and I had faced any kind of issue together, and his response was to call me a liar and leave without really talking about it. He clearly hadn't thought to offer me any comfort, or even to ask how I felt about the whole situation.

TWO DAYS LATER, I STILL hadn't heard from Dan. I decided to put myself out of my misery and text him. I spent twenty minutes composing a "short, breezy" text, and another five working up the courage to send it. In the end I just closed my eyes and pressed the send button without letting myself think about it any further, my hands shaking. It was nothing – I had just said "hey Dan, just checking in! How's your week going?" – but it was his reply I was scared about. I still wasn't very happy with him about the way he had handled it all, but I did see potential there and I didn't want it to end.

A few minutes passed before my phone pinged. I had literally thrown my phone to the side on my couch after sending the message, refusing to look at it again until I heard the message come through. My hands were still shaking as I picked it up, but his reply told me nothing. "Not bad", it said simply. He didn't ask how I was, or expand on anything. It didn't give me a lot to work with, but I replied anyway. I needed to know, one way or another, which way this was going to go. "Do you want to come over tonight?" I asked, holding my breath as I typed.

There was another gut-wrenching wait before my phone lit up again. "I'm sorry," the message said, and I squeezed my eyes shut momentarily. "I don't think we can make it work."

I nodded to myself, as if Dan was there in the room with me. It was what I'd been expecting for the last few days, but it still stung. Not to mention, he was breaking up with me through text? Had he read the Douchebag Manual or something?

My fingers hovered over my phone before I replied. A thousand replies went through my mind, everything from sentimental to scathing. In the end, I kept it simple, just like he had. "Good luck to you, then," I wrote, and just like that, I was single again.

# Chapter 42

I spent the next week wallowing, but I knew it wasn't really Dan I was upset about. It was the idea of him, the possibility of the security a relationship would have offered. It certainly wasn't the feminist ideal I'd always aimed to keep up, but I was lonely. Sure, I had great friends and a baby of my own, and I should be thankful for all of that, and of course I was. Deep down, though, I just wanted what Carrie had with John, what Jack was beginning to have with Nathan. It seemed to come so easily for some people. Carrie had been on precisely *one* date with another man – well, boy, really, given she was in high school at the time – before she'd met her knight in shining armour. Jack had obviously had his share of duds in the past, but having a seven-month-old baby didn't seem to create any obstacle towards *him* finding a guy to have a relationship with. I, on the other hand, was at home eating M&Ms straight from the packet until I felt sick, counteracting them with some corn chips because I needed something savoury, and following that with more M&Ms as a chaser. It wasn't really the dream life of a woman in her thirties.

On the plus side, I definitely wasn't pregnant. I'd taken three more pregnancy tests and they'd all shown up negative. That was one complication I definitely didn't need right now, despite my momentary hormonal lapse when I'd first had the pregnancy scare.

Eight days after things officially ended with Dan, I decided I'd wallowed long enough. I'd given myself a week and even though I couldn't say I was 100 percent over him, I was going to convince myself to move on. I got up early and took Lexie out for a walk, jogging intermittently as I pushed her along in her pram. The exercise and the music blasting through my earphones helped take my mind off things, and gave me a handy rush of endorphins, so by the time I got home I was feeling a lot more cheerful. I decided to continue my good mood by having a cook-up. I ended up making lasagne, a chicken curry and eggplant parmigiana, giving us meals for the next few days as well as some options to freeze. I felt good, like I was getting my life back on track. The September school holidays were approaching, so I lined up a few kid-friendly dates with Carrie and Georgia for the next week, and was in the middle of dusting the furniture with music pumping loudly when Jack got home.

"Well!" he laughed, looking at me in surprise. "You're looking... good." It was basically the understatement of the year, at least in comparison to how I'd been. It was important to remember that the last time he'd seen me I'd been surrounded by food packets and empty soft drink cans. Even ignoring the fact that I was willingly cleaning for once, the improvement must have been surprising. He came in and kissed Lexie on the head, then pulled his tie off with relish. It seemed to be the male equivalent of coming home and taking your bra off.

"I feel good," I told him honestly. "I've decided to *wash that man right out of my hair.*" I did an exaggerated dance move as I sang, for Alexis' benefit. "He's not worth crying over, so I'm being a good little 1950s housewife for my gay bestie and his boyfriend."

"I'm not sure there was much of that happening in the '50s," Jack said wryly, "but good for you! You can shine my shoes while you're at it."

I did a little curtsy. "And peel your grapes, sir?"

We laughed together and he offered to set the table while I continued to clean. We normally ate on the couch in front of the TV, but Jack said that such a nice-looking meal deserved the full table treatment. "Nathan's on a late shift, so it's just the two of us. Well, three," he added, nodding towards our daughter.

I smiled. "A family dinner will be nice," I said. As soon as the words were out of my mouth, I realised they could sound like I was excluding Nathan from our family, but Jack didn't seem bothered.

We sat down at the table together, Lexie in her high chair. She'd only recently started using it and still wasn't a huge fan of being confined, but it seemed like the thing to do while we were sitting around the table together. Jack started talking about his day, filling me in on the issues he was having with his supervisor. Jack had been close with his previous boss, but since she moved on, he'd been struggling with the new guy, who seemed to go out of his way to make Jack's life worse. "I'm thinking of looking elsewhere," he said, and I nodded in support. "I think that's probably a good idea," I told him. "You haven't been happy there for a while." I paused. "Speaking of work," I said slowly, "Ann-Marie contacted me today." I had been surprised to get the call from my Principal, and even more surprised when I heard what she had to say.

"Oh, yeah? Something about next year?" he asked. I'd officially spoken to Ann-Marie about six weeks ago, telling her my decision to go back full-time the following year. I knew it would be a challenge, balancing work with a one-year-old, but I was ready for it.

"No, actually, about next term," I said. "The Year 4 teacher has had to go part-time for family reasons. Ann-Marie wondered if I would be willing to teach two days a week." I was strangely nervous telling him. These sorts of decisions used to be mine alone to make, even if I ran them by Jack and the girls for their input first. Now, it seemed like everything was a joint decision. I knew Jack felt it, too, that his casual talk of searching for a new job was also a way of feeling out my reaction over it. It was like having a husband, in a way. All the decisions we made had to be for the good of our family unit. It wasn't just about me anymore. I wasn't entirely sure how I felt about that.

"Oh, wow!" Jack exclaimed, looking up at me in surprise. "Is that something you'd be interested in?" He asked this part carefully, seemingly unsure of how he was supposed to react.

"Honestly, I'm... kind of excited about it," I said. "I've never taught Year 4 before, but I've always wanted to. Plus, it'd be a good way to feel things out before I go back full-time. You know I've been a bit worried about that." I'd seen first-hand with Carrie and Georgia how hard it could be to balance teaching and parenting. It was getting easier for Georgia now Mike was older, but I'd been around when Carrie's kids were born and I'd seen how difficult it was for her to miss their school assemblies, or to always have to come in when she was sick herself because she'd used all of her sick leave up for Lachlan or Aria's illnesses. I filled Jack in briefly on some of the challenges they faced.

Jack frowned. "Isn't that all the more reason to put it off as long as possible?"

"That's one way to look at it," I conceded. "But it's September now. I can keep stressing until next January, and then jump in head first, or I can ease myself into it now. Two days a week feels manageable, so it might just make it less scary when I have to do it for five. Plus, this way I'll get a bit of holiday pay," I added tantalisingly. My maternity leave had already run out, and although Jack's wage was enough to pay the bills, it left little room for fun.

He shrugged. "It's your decision, babe. If you're happy, I'm happy. What will we do with Lexie?" I appreciated the use of *we* rather than *you*.

"I was going to check with Mum," I replied. She'd always offered to look after her only grandchild as much as was needed, so I couldn't imagine a couple of days a week would be an issue. "It's Thursday and Friday by the way, so no staff meetings, and I'd only need to plan for what I teach on those two days, so I should be right to leave by four each day."

Jack laughed. "You sound like you're trying to convince me. What did you say to Ann-Marie?"

"I told her I'd have to check with you and Mum and get back to her, but I did tell her I was interested. She seemed pretty happy with that." We had a limited pool of relief teachers at the school so she couldn't rely on one of them, and I knew if I could save her doing interviews, she would be happy about that. Of course, I also liked to imagine she was eager to get me back for me, not just for convenience.

"Well, it's fine with me," Jack shrugged. "It'll be an adjustment, but I think you're right – a couple of days a week will be easier than going full-time straight away. Just see what your mum says, and we can go from there."

I nodded, smiling. I'd already decided to look into day care if Mum wasn't willing to mind Lexie, since that was our plan for the following year anyway. One way or another, I was going back to work.

# Chapter 43

Mum seemed happy when I asked about minding her grandchild, and Carrie and Georgia were ecstatic to hear I was coming back to work sooner than expected. "Friday coffee dates!!" Carrie messaged, and I laughed. I used to be the one trying to coax her out after school on a Friday. If I'd wanted proof she'd missed having me at work, this was it!

I met up with Kathleen, the teacher I would be job-sharing with, over the holidays. She told me how her adult daughter was having some health issues and Kathleen had offered to reduce her workload so she could help her out. We talked over the curriculum together, and came away with a plan – in addition to Maths and English, which were done daily, I would take charge of teaching the entirety of the Health, Visual Arts and History units, and would help with the report card marks for those subjects. It seemed like a pretty fair way to go about things. I wasn't used to job sharing, but it seemed easier to step into someone else's classroom than it would have been to relinquish my own class for a day or two each week. I remained oddly excited about the challenge.

The two weeks of holidays passed quickly, as they always do, and before I knew it, it was the first Wednesday night of Term 4, the night before my return to work. I was stalking around the house in a bad mood, slamming cupboard doors and generally not being a pleasure to be around. I saw Nathan glaring my way a few times, but he didn't say anything. Finally, Jack took the bait. "Are we okay there, Annie?" he asked mildly, picking Lexie up and approaching me in the kitchen the way a lion tamer might approach a particularly out-of-control animal.

"Fine," I snapped, pushing past him towards the fridge.

"I'm surprised you didn't get something stronger," he said, nodding towards the bottle of water I'd just pulled out. "What's the matter?"

I sighed and slumped against the cupboard. "Nothing. Sorry. I'm just in a shitty mood because I have to go back tomorrow."

To his credit, Jack managed not to look like he wanted to murder me, but there was a distinct tone of exasperation in his voice when he replied. "I thought you were excited to go back?"

"I was! I am. Well, I'm not. I don't know," I said, aware of the whiny note I could hear as I spoke. "I thought I was looking forward to it, and I'm excited to see everyone again, but then reality comes around and it's just so hard to leave her. It's different to going out on girls' nights. It seems so much more..." I searched for the right word. "Permanent."

"Oh, honey, I know. It's still hard for me to leave her every morning! But you'll be fine. You're a great teacher, and it's only two days a week. Plus, you'll see more of Carrie and Georgia," he added. He knew the girls could always cheer me up.

I was just starting to feel better when I heard Nathan mutter something from the couch. "What was that?" I demanded, swinging around to stare at him.

"Nothing," Nathan growled in response.

"Well it wasn't nothing, because you said *something*," I snapped. I was obviously still spoiling for a fight. "What was it?"

Nathan rolled his eyes. "I just think you're being a bit of a drama queen about a situation you invented. No one asked you to go back to work, and it's only two days a week, for God's sake! Some of us have to go in every day, and you don't hear us complaining."

My heart started racing, angry heat prickling behind my eyes. "Yeah, because staying at home with an infant is so *easy*, I forgot! I'd love to see you try it, Nathan."

"Okay, okay," Jack tried to interject, but Nathan spoke over him, his voice getting louder.

"Please! Like you're not watching hours of trashy TV every day."

My voice grew into a growl of frustration. "You have *no* idea what I do every day! I cook a hot meal every bloody day, and I don't hear you complaining. I'm not making it for you, I'm making it for *my family*, but you're always the first to hoe into it. I clean, and yeah, I look after the baby, who's supposed to be a priority for all of us but who clearly isn't for you!" By the end of my tirade I was basically shouting. Although there had always been an undercurrent of tension between us, this was the first time Nathan and I had argued so openly. I was tense, but it felt surprisingly good to get some of these things off my chest.

Nathan laughed bitterly. "Your family," he repeated. "You mean my boyfriend? The one you want but can't have? That family?"

I heard Jack take a sharp intake of breath. I felt like I'd been slapped across the face. "I don't *want* him," I protested, my voice sounding weak even to my own ears. "I know he's your boyfriend, but I was around before you and I'll be around after you, too."

"Guys, you need to stop," I heard Jack plead. "Both of you. This isn't good for any of us." As if on cue, Lexie started to wail, and Jack held her closer.

Hearing my daughter's cries caused all the fight to go out of me. I hated it when she was upset. I didn't want to keep screaming at Nathan until I was hoarse, and I had no interest in hearing anything he had to say to me. "Are you right with her?" I asked Jack softly. "I'm going to my room." I headed upstairs without waiting for an answer.

I had no sooner closed my bedroom door than the tears I'd been expecting came. I kept myself closed up in my room all night. I heard Jack knock softly on my door before he went to bed, but I pretended to be asleep. I wasn't angry at Jack, but I simply couldn't face him right now. I ended up sending Nathan an apology text, and he responded in kind. I wasn't sure his response was any more sincere than mine was, but I knew we had to move past this if we were going to keep living together. I didn't want to upset Jack, and I couldn't stand living with awkward confrontation myself.

If I was being truly honest, though, I had a more important need to set things right with Nathan.

If things continued this way, and Jack ended up having to choose between the two of us, I had no idea which one he would choose. And I wasn't sure I wanted to find out.

# Chapter 44

The one benefit of all the drama the night before was that going back to work seemed positively easy in comparison. Mum's house was on the way to work, so I'd arranged to drop Lexie off on my way in. Leaving her was hard, but it wasn't as tough as I'd expected it might be. I knew I would see her again in just a few short hours, and she was in good hands with my mother. We had to have our mobiles off in class, so I told Mum to call the school if there were any emergencies, and after depositing what felt like a thousand kisses on my daughter's cheeks, I finally headed off.

I had left home early, partly to reduce my stress by arriving at school as early as possible and partly to avoid seeing Nathan. Even with the baby hand-over, I was in my classroom by 7.20. I sat at the desk and looked over the class list, trying to familiarise myself with the names and figure out how to pronounce some of the trickier ones. I'd taught a lot of the students at the school but by changing year levels I'd managed to miss this lot, so I wasn't overly familiar with many of them except the "high flyers" of the group. My next step was to look over my plans for the day, hoping to get to know them backwards and forwards. I'd always been willing to fly by the seat of my pants as a teacher, but having not set foot inside a classroom since the previous December, I wanted to make things as foolproof as possible. Only once I felt confident about what I was doing with my day did I head over to the staffroom to put my lunch away. I knew my well-meaning colleagues wouldn't let me out of there once they'd seen me. Sure enough, everyone seemed thrilled to see me, greeting me like a long-lost friend. I met the few people who had started work there during my leave period, and eventually Georgia came stumbling into the staffroom, pushing her sunglasses up on her head and throwing her multitude of bags down on the table before rushing over for an enthusiastic hug.

"One week, Georgia," I laughed, pulling away. "It's been *one week* since we've seen each other."

"Yes, but it's been way too long since I've seen you *here!*" my friend squealed. "I'm so glad to have you back!"

Carrie's greeting was similarly enthusiastic, if more laid-back in nature. Uncharacteristically, I hadn't filled them in on last night's fight via messenger, so when Carrie suggested we go to Grindtime after school to dissect the day, I was eager to agree. Of course, first I had to survive the school day.

As it turned out, I needn't have worried. My students were, for the most part, delightful, and I loved their independence, compared with the younger year levels I was used to. By the end of the day I had a handle on most of their names – I'd always been quick at picking them up – and I'd started making some headway on their History unit, which discussed famous explorers. I was pleased with how naturally teaching seemed to come back to me. Just like riding a bike, although having attempted to ride a bike in adulthood a couple of years ago, I could vouch for the fact that it didn't actually come back to you the way the cliché promises it will.

I'd never thought the school day went quickly before but somehow, the 3pm bell was ringing before I knew it. I smiled at the children as I wished them a good afternoon, and spent the next half hour tidying up and getting myself ready for the next day. Carrie came in as I was using the photocopier in the staffroom. "Grindtime?" she asked eagerly, wiggling her eyebrows up and down, and I nodded. "I'm nearly finished here. Call Georgia and I'm ready to head off whenever."

Ten minutes later we were sitting together at Grindtime, just like old times. The first thing they wanted to hear about was my new class, so I filled them in on how my day had gone. "They're a lot more independent than the little ones, obviously, but I didn't get a single picture drawn for me, and no hugs. I even read them a story and not one of them tried to tickle my feet," I laughed, referring to the well-known teacher hazard that came with working in the younger years.

"Sounds successful," Carrie commented. "And you were okay with leaving Lexie?" Both of my friends were familiar with how difficult it was to leave your kids to go back to work. Georgia had been halfway through her teaching degree when she had Michael, but she was determined not to let her studies lapse and had returned to uni when he was only a year old, with a part-time job to pay the bills. I didn't know how she'd managed it, but I was glad she had. The world needed more teachers like Georgia. Carrie, of course, had a few years' teaching experience under her belt before she got married and had Lachie and Aria, all three events within four years of each other. Having more teaching experience should make it easier to go back after having kids, but I wasn't so sure at this stage. The thing with teaching is that every year is a different kind of challenge, even if you've been doing the job for twenty years, because it all comes down to the kids in your class. I seemed to have been blessed with a pretty good group for this term, but I knew enough not to count on that remaining to be true.

"It was okay," I answered. "Honestly, it was kind of all a rush between getting ready and getting her off to Mum. The hardest thing is the lack of sleep." They nodded in silent understanding. Lexie was a reasonable sleeper, but I still had at least one wake-up a night – usually more, since I often woke up in a panic just to check on her if I *didn't* hear her cry. And of course, I'd been up by five AM to make sure I got out the door on time. "I didn't get as much sleep as usual last night even aside from motherhood," I added, filling them in briefly on my fight with Nathan. I always appreciated how outraged my friends looked on my behalf when I told them stories like that. We all paid out on each other a lot, but I knew they would always have my back about the things that mattered. "That bastard!" Georgia exclaimed when I'd finished recounting the previous night's events.

I nodded sadly. "I know I was to blame, too – I was in a foul mood! But I'm really worried about what it means going forward."

"You were in a foul mood because you were worried about going back to work for the first time," Carrie said pragmatically. "That's totally understandable! He could have cut you some slack." Georgia nodded emphatically, still frowning. "Besides, even if you were a total bitch to him, saying you have feelings for Jack is so out of line."

"You guys did kiss and make up, though, right?" Carrie asked.

"Sort of, yeah. Just a quick apology text each, I haven't seen him in person since the fight. I think it'll still be a bit awkward, but I'm glad we at least said that we're sorry." I gave a hollow laugh. "I'm not sure either of us really meant it, though."

"I'm sure everything will be fine," Georgia said sympathetically. "He's not the type to hold a grudge, is he?"

I shrugged. To be honest, I still didn't feel like I knew Nathan all that well, even though we were living together. I never would have expected that he'd blow up at me the way he had. I was being honest when I said I knew I shouldered some of the blame, but if he'd just kept quiet my bad mood would have blown over after a few kind words from Jack.

"It's not like I can turn back time," I said. "We'll just have to work on our relationship a bit more moving forward. It's what I've been meaning to do, anyway." Nathan and I might never become best friends, but he might end up being in my daughter's life forever. For Jack's sake and for Lexie's, we had to make something work.

# Chapter 45

My second day of teaching was less successful than my first. My main behavioural issue, a boy named Xavier, flew into a rage about some small indiscretion by another student and flipped a chair over, screaming and swearing at the top of his voice. The kids, having been in a class with him for the majority of the year, were clearly more used to this behaviour than I was, and after my lengthy break from teaching I was fairly shaken up by it. Later on, I climbed up on the bench to hang some of the kids' work on the pinboard and fell off when I was trying to slide down, bruising my knee instantly. It hurt a hell of a lot, and the worst part was I couldn't even complain since climbing on a bench was up there with the most heinous of crimes you could commit from a workplace health and safety perspective. In the afternoon, the Internet stopped working, rendering my planned Health lesson completely useless. I'd always been good at improvising – in fact, there had been times in the classroom when I would literally open my mouth to start a sentence with no idea of what I was going to say until I said it. Thinking on your feet was a valuable part of the teacher toolbox. Now, though, I was out of practice and I had to resort to lamely making the kids clean the classroom for ten minutes while I tried to think of something worthwhile they could do.

By the end of the day, I was more than ready to relax on the couch with a wine, content in the knowledge that I didn't have to go back to work until the following Thursday. I left a brief note for Kathleen, my job-share partner, about a writing activity they had started but not finished and decided to do some printing for the following week before making an early getaway. I knew I'd need to start pulling some longer hours pretty soon or I'd fall behind, but right now I just wanted to get home to my baby.

As it so often does, life had different ideas. My classroom phone rang, the jangling tone jolting me out of my work. "Hello?" I said into the phone, my fingers still flying over the keyboard of my laptop.

"Hey." It was Carrie's voice – we'd long since stopped identifying ourselves over the phone to each other. "Are you free? Can you stop by my classroom before you head home?"

I frowned. "Sure, but is everything okay?"

"Yeah, it's okay." She sounded breathless, though, and I knew something was up. My mind instantly went to John and the kids. "I'll be right over," I said, grabbing all my things and making a hasty exit. Carrie's classroom was on the other side of the school, but I got there as quickly as I could. I needed to make sure everything was okay.

When I got there Carrie was sitting behind her desk, looking dazed. "What is it?" I cried as I burst through her classroom door.

She smiled faintly as she saw my panicked face. "Sorry, I didn't mean to scare you! I'm just a bit..." She paused. "I interviewed at St Catherine's a few days ago, and they just called to tell me I got the job."

My stomach lurched. I'd known Carrie had been keeping an eye out for jobs closer to home for the last couple of years, but she hadn't told me she was at the interview stage. Even though I'd always known we couldn't work together forever, I'd pushed the thought of us separating out of my mind. I'd relied on Carrie in my teaching career for so long, I couldn't imagine not being with her.

"Congratulations!" I managed to say, running over and giving her a hug. I was so happy for her, knowing how much easier the reduced travel time would make it for her and her family. St Catherine's was the school Lachie was at, and where Aria would be commencing the following year. Her kids were pretty well-behaved and Carrie was a dream parent for any teacher to have in their class, so I wasn't surprised they had snapped her up. Of course, none of that made it any easier to picture working without her. Thank God I still had Georgia.

"I'm sorry I didn't tell you about the interview," Carrie said softly, and I suspected my emotions were written across my face. "I didn't think anything would come of it, so I didn't want to upset you for no reason."

I shook my head, smiling slightly. Carrie had always been too hard on herself, so I wasn't surprised she'd expected not to be successful. "I'm so happy for you," I said, truthfully. "It'll just be so weird without my work wife!"

She nodded, laughing a little even as tears came to her eyes. "I'm going to miss you so much, Annie. You're the best work wife ever," she added, clearly trying to lighten the mood a little bit.

Her tears were contagious, and I found myself wiping at my own eyes. "Meanwhile, thank goodness I came back to work early! Can you imagine?"

"I thought the same thing!" she exclaimed. "If you'd stayed on leave 'til next year, I just would have been... gone. Never to work together again," she added, mock dramatically.

"Have you told Georgia yet?" I asked, knowing what the answer would be. Although the three of us were a tight-knit group, if Carrie had news, I knew she would always come to me first.

She shook her head. "I have to break it to her, but I wanted to make sure you were the first to know. I'm only about to go tell Ann-Marie now, so please don't tell a soul."

"Of course," I vowed, pretending to zip my lips, and then paused. "'A soul' doesn't include Jack, does it?"

# Chapter 46

By the time I picked Alexis up and made it home, it was nearly 5:30. I knew I should start making dinner but instead I sat Lexie down on her floor mat and pulled out her blocks, starting a game with her. Only two days of work done, and I was exhausted. The surprise of the afternoon's news hadn't helped. I felt ready to crawl into bed already. It hit me that the inability to look after yourself when you were having a crappy day was probably the biggest drawback to parenthood. Pre-Lexie, if I was struggling through a Friday, I would have had a couple of drinks out with friends, or just put on my favourite movie to help me forget the outside world for a while. Now, my priority was looking after Lexie, not looking after myself.

As if on cue, my daughter giggled as she knocked some blocks over. I smiled fondly at her. Leave it to Alexis to remind me that the drawbacks of parenthood were nothing compared to the benefits.

SINCE CARRIE HAD GIVEN approval for my "faux-husband" to know her news, I filled him (and, by default, Nathan) in on her new job over dinner that night.

"Oh, that's a surprise! How do you feel about it?" Jack asked. He knew how tight my bond with Carrie was, and I loved how great he was at always asking how I felt about things, rather than jumping straight into a reaction. I always told him he should be a therapist.

"Mixed feelings," I replied honestly. "I'm so happy for her, and I know how much easier it will make everything for the kids. Plus, she's been at Fallen Oaks her whole career, so it's time for a change." By that token it was time for a change for me as well, but I couldn't begin to think about that while Lexie was still young. "But I can't even picture school without her. I don't think we'll fall out of touch or anything – I mean, I'm her daughter's godmother! But it won't be the same as seeing her every day."

Jack nodded. "I guess you just make the most of the time you do have together, and make sure to see each other as regularly as you can next year."

"Or maybe it's not all about you," Nathan muttered tightly.

My blood ran cold. Nathan and I had been keeping up a polite, if slightly cold, façade since our fight two nights earlier, but now he seemed to be itching for round two. I wrestled for a minute between taking the bait or being the bigger person and ignoring him, and I astounded myself by deciding to take the high road.

Even more astounding, it was Jack who responded. "Drop it, Nathan," he said, a note of warning in his voice. My heart leapt. Jack had always been non-confrontational, and even though we'd fought a few times throughout the year I didn't expect him to ever argue back on my behalf. Hearing him speak up for me, even mildly, meant a lot.

Nathan shook his head but kept his mouth closed, his lips tight. He took another forkful of dinner and for a moment, everything was silent.

I tried not to say anything, but the words flew from my lips as if I was possessed. "I know it's not all about me, Nathan," I said bitterly, not meeting his eyes.

He shrugged. "Your friend got a great opportunity and instead of taking five minutes to be happy for her, you're whinging about how it's going to affect you. Sure *sounds* like it's all about you."

The words stung, but I couldn't even deny they were true. My first reaction had been to think about myself. Having said that, I didn't think even Carrie would blame me if she knew how I felt. If I was the one who had taken on another job first, I would have been surprised if Carrie didn't feel some misgivings about me leaving. Nathan simply didn't have a friendship with anyone that was as close as Carrie's and mine, and I told him so.

"Yeah, that's why," he said sarcastically. "I'm not as good a friend as you are. I guess that's why I actually consider my friends' feelings, instead of always acting like everything they do is a slight against me." He shook his head again and muttered "unbelievable" under his breath.

I felt like I'd been slapped. I was hurt and frustrated, but there was something deeper to it. For the first time, I realised that Nathan and I didn't just have our little differences – he genuinely disliked me as a person, and the feeling was mutual. It wasn't simply the stress of living together when we didn't know each other all that well. We fundamentally disliked each other, and I wasn't sure if anything would ever change that. I wasn't sure how to deal with that.

I put my fork down on my plate and stood up from the table. "I think I'm going to take Lexie for her bath," I said quietly, moving away without another word.

I managed to avoid the boys fairly successfully, until there was a knock on my door a couple of hours later. I had put Lexie to bed and was lying on my bed, reading. When Jack opened the door and pushed his way in, I pointed silently to our sleeping baby, giving Jack the hint to keep as quiet as possible.

He came and sat down on the bed beside me. "Are you okay?" he asked softly.

I nodded, grateful that he'd come to check on me. "I guess things aren't all rosy here, are they?"

Jack hesitated for a moment, then put his hand on my leg. "I just wish you'd dropped it."

That took me by surprise. "*I'd* dropped it? Nathan started it," I protested, aware that I sounded like a ten-year-old.

"He did start it," Jack agreed, "but he was also perfectly willing to stop after I told him to. You're the one who turned it into something more."

I thought of how Jack had stood up for me, and I mentally kicked myself for not letting it end there. He was right; I knew it took a lot for Jack to fight back, and he'd been willing to step in on my behalf. I should have been grateful, instead of insisting on arguing back with Nathan myself.

Just like that, all the defensiveness went out of me. "I'm sorry," I whispered. "You're right, you were just trying to keep the peace. I should have kept my mouth shut."

Jack looked down. "Don't be too hard on yourself. Nathan did start it, just like you said," he added gently. "I just don't want all this fighting to keep on. You and Nathan are both pretty stubborn when you want to be, you know." This line caused a snort of laughter from me. "Sooner or later, at least one of you has to decide to be the bigger person, or none of this is going to work."

"You're right," I admitted. "I'm going to try, I promise. I don't want to live with all of this conflict any more than you do."

Jack regarded me seriously. "I don't want to have joint custody of Lexie. I want us to stay together, like we'd always planned. But I want to be with Nathan, too, so if it's not going to work then we might need to look at some other options."

I nodded, feeling a lump forming in my throat. Just as I'd always feared, Jack had basically told me that if it came down to a choice between Nathan and me, I'd be the one out on my own. Part of me had expected it, but another part was surprised. It had been Jack and Annie for so long, I thought our bond was stronger than that.

# Chapter 47

True to my word, I started letting the little things go with Nathan. Jack must have given him a similar lecture, because I noticed he'd also stopped picking fights with me. We became less competitive. He'd also picked up some extra shifts at the hospital which definitely helped, since we were spending less time together. I wasn't sure if it was a deliberate action or a coincidence, but either way, I was happy. The tone of the whole house felt lighter, and I could tell Jack was pleased not to have conflict between his boyfriend and his best friend. Things seemed to slowly be getting better.

It wasn't just the home situation that was improving. Lexie was growing and learning new things by the day. I loved watching her develop further and further into a real little girl, rather than a baby. She had taken her first steps, and seemed eager to start making her way own way around in the world. She was playing and laughing more than she ever had before, and I absolutely loved seeing the world expand for her. My favourite time of the day was playing games with her. I had finally booked into the mothers' group that I'd tried so early on, which met, conveniently enough, on a Wednesday afternoon. I was eager to give Lexie some playtime with kids her own age, but I was equally happy to have some adults to talk to who were at the same stage as I was.

The day of the mothers' group meeting (or "catch up", as the group apparently liked to call it), I dressed Lexie in my favourite of her dresses, a little white one with cherries all over it and a bright red bow across the middle. I snapped a photo for Jack, who quickly replied with a text telling his "favourite girls" to enjoy themselves. When we arrived at the local park where mothers' group was meeting, a woman came bustling over to me. "You must be our new member!" she exclaimed, with a hint of an American accent. "I'm Erica. Welcome to our group! I'll come and introduce you." She took us over and listed the names of the other five women and the eight kids who were there with them. I knew I wouldn't remember any of them, but I smiled and said hi to everyone, then let Lexie out of her pram. "Come and meet the others!" I said cheerfully, squatting down to the picnic blanket. The kids ranged in ages, but the oldest looked to be about three. Once Alexis was settled on the picnic blanket with the other kids, I joined the other women. A couple of them were deep in conversation and barely noticed me, while another was watching her son's every move intently, but the woman next to me smiled warmly. "I'm Sarah," she said, and I recognised her name from the email when Lexie was so little. "That's my son, Jasper," she added, pointing at a boy of about two who was playing near Lexie.

"Is he your only one?" I asked, and Sarah laughed. "I've actually got a fifteen-year-old as well, Jasper's half-brother."

"Wow!" Not only did Sarah look far too young to have a child that old, I couldn't imagine going back and doing it all again when Lexie was a teenager. "Hat's off to you, I guess," I laughed. "I think one might be the limit for me."

"Your partner doesn't want any more?" she ventured – a risky question, I thought, given that I'd referred to "me" rather than "us".

"We talked about maybe going back, but it's been a little rougher than I thought," I admitted. There was no need to explain the whole situation with Jack to a woman I barely knew. Naturally, I then found myself following the guilty mothers' handbook and adding "but I wouldn't change it for the world!" I was somewhat disgusted with myself for becoming such a cliché. I could only imagine what Julie would say if she could hear me. We always used to laugh together at some of the things mothers on the Internet said, even though I was nursing a desperate desire to become one of them. Our favourite was when they made comments such as "as a mother, I think it's devastating when a child goes missing". Julie loved to screenshot such comments when she found them, sending them to me with sarcastic quips like "shit! As a non-parent, I think it's awesome when kids go missing!" and "I don't have children, so I lack the mental capacity to realise this is bad".

Sarah nodded. "You don't have to tell me twice! I never thought I'd have another one, but my husband really wanted one of his own. Well, he wanted three of his own, but I'm hoping I can convince him to stop with Jasper. He's such a ratbag," she added, looking affectionately at her son.

Sarah and I chatted easily for another half hour or so before she stood up. "I'm sorry to leave," she said, "but I start night shift at six. I have to drop her off to my mother-in-law's."

"It was lovely to meet you," I said honestly. I hadn't felt such a natural, easy connection with someone on first meeting since meeting Georgia.

"I'll give you my number, if you want," Sarah offered, and we swapped phones and entered our details. "I'll see you at next week's catch up, but feel free to text anytime."

The other mums and I waved Sarah and Jasper off and turned our attention back to the kids. Lexie looked happy, but I knew I would have to take her home soon to get her bathed and fed. It was nearly five. Lexie took a few tottering steps towards me, which I took as a sign to pack her up and say my goodbyes to the other mums. "This was so great," I told them as I was grabbing the last of my things. "It's so nice to have kids her own age for her to play with – not to mention adult company for me!"

"We loved having you!" Erica said, and the other women nodded and smiled in agreement. I walked off, wheeling Lexie in the pram while I balanced the rest of my things.

We'd only driven five minutes away from the park when a car pulled out in front of me, too close. I slammed the brakes on, breathing a sigh of relief at the near miss and thumping my fist down on the horn. "Jackass," I muttered, and then screamed out as a car flew into the side of mine.

# Chapter 48

Lexie's cry was instantaneous and piercing. I whipped my head around to look at her, relieved to see that she looked okay, for now at least. I knew she could have internal injuries that wouldn't show up yet. I continued staring at her, dazed, before finally having the sense to pull the car slowly off onto the side of the road. The man in the other car did the same and we got out of our cars at the same time. I opened up the door beside my daughter, ready to pull her out.

"Are you okay?" he called out, jogging up to me. He glanced at my car and noticed Alexis, still crying, in her car seat. "Oh, shit," he muttered.

I nodded, tears filling my eyes. "Oh, shit" just about covered it. It was only the second car accident I'd ever been in, and it was exponentially more terrifying with my baby in the backseat. I went to pull her out, but the man stopped me. "I'm going to call an ambulance," he said. "Just leave her there for the moment. It's safest for her."

I stared at Lexie, wondering if he was right. All I wanted to do was hold her in my arms, but I didn't want to cause any further harm if she had internal injuries. In the end I decided to be cautious and leave her in there, even if it nearly broke my heart to do so. I leant in, gently stroking her cheeks and whispering to her that she would be okay.

The man, Jason, and I exchanged details while we waited, but I was shaking through the entire exchange. I wanted to get it done, though. When the ambulance finally arrived, I wanted to be free to get onboard as quickly as humanly possible.

Fortunately, the ambulance was there within a few minutes, although I was so anxious it felt much longer. I stood back and watched as the paramedics lifted Lexie carefully out and examined her, a sight I knew I would never forget. A young paramedic came over to me.

"Your daughter looks to be fine," she assured me, "but we would like to take her to the hospital, to get her looked over properly, just in case." I nodded and she continued "Come on-board with us." She gestured over to where the tow truck had already got into position, ready to take my car. Where were all these tow trucks lurking, just waiting for an emergency? They always seemed to arrive almost instantaneously.

I nodded. "Yes, of course."

"And how are you, Mum?" she added as we finally got on board the ambulance. It felt like a lifetime had passed, but it could only have been twenty minutes since the accident.

"I feel okay. I guess I'll be sore in the morning, but nothing seems too damaged." I didn't really care about myself. Lexie was my only priority. Speaking of which...

"Can I use my phone?" I asked, and she nodded her assent.

I tried Jack immediately, but his phone went straight to voicemail. I knew he would be in a meeting and that of course he had no idea what had happened, but I was still irrationally angry at him for not being available to his daughter. Next, I called Carrie. "Lexie and I were in a car crash," I gasped down the phone, so quickly it might as well have all been one word. "I'm in the ambulance on the way to hospital now."

"Oh, my God!" Carrie's normally calm voice rose in shock. "Are you okay?"

"We're both okay," I said. "I think so, anyway." I choked back a sob.

Carrie hesitated. "I'm about to go to Lachie's school play, but if you need me, I can see what I can do," she offered.

My heart sank. I had known about the school play, but it had completely slipped my mind with everything that had happened. I knew her offer was genuine, but I also knew how much she would hate to miss Lachlan's play – not to mention, it was a good opportunity for her future colleagues to see her supporting the school. I couldn't possibly let her do that for me. "No, it's okay," I replied with a conviction I didn't really feel. "It's not like there's anything you can really do, anyway. We're fine, honestly."

I felt deflated as I hung up. I didn't want to be alone, but I couldn't ask Georgia to come to a hospital with me, not after everything she'd been through. Mum and Dad were out of town, and I knew Julie had a date tonight.

I tried Jack again, but his phone went straight through to voicemail once more. I decided to call the radio station directly. I didn't really care what the meeting was about, they could interrupt it for this.

"I'm sorry," said the clipped voice of the receptionist when I finally got through to an actual person. "Jack Delaney has left for the day."

I closed my eyes. "Well, do you know any way I can reach him? It's an emergency. With his daughter," I added for good measure.

The receptionist paused. "Only his mobile, but I assume you've tried that. I'm sorry, I don't know what to tell you."

"It's okay," I said, even though it was anything but. We pulled up to the hospital just as I hung up.

I expected the scene to be like something out of the many hospital dramas I'd watched over the years, but everything was calmer, more sedate. It put my mind slightly at ease. It didn't seem quite as scary without doctors running around wheeling gurneys, screaming *stat* and looking frantic.

I was directed to a waiting room where I filled out a form and then just sat, holding Lexie on my lap. She was calmer now, and she wound her tiny fist around my thumb. I bent down to kiss her forehead, taking long, deep breaths to try to calm myself.

It's a lonely life, sometimes, being single. I certainly wasn't going to get any Nobel Prizes for that original thought, but I generally felt happier with my life than most single people seemed to be. I knew so many people who couldn't stand to be alone, but I've always been fairly happy in my own company. I actually really enjoy going to movies alone or even sitting in a restaurant by myself, as long as I have a book. That said, I'm only human, and there are times when it gets to me more than others. Sitting there, in the hospital waiting room, my body curled around Lexie's... I'd never felt more alone.

# Chapter 49

The jangling of my phone startled me. I was in the hospital ward, getting checked over by a doctor. They'd already examined Lexie and, thank God, had declared her to be entirely unharmed. I had no idea how, when the impact had been so close to her, but I was willing to accept it as a miracle.

I looked at the phone and saw Jack's name light up the screen. I pointed at it, asking the doctor if I could take it. "Quickly," he responded.

I heard the panic in Jack's voice instantly. "What happened?" he asked breathlessly once I had told him we were at the hospital.

I made sure to tell him we were both fine, before filling him in on the accident. "We're just about to leave here, if you can come and get us?" I finished up.

"Oh, my God, I feel terrible," Jack cried. "My phone mustn't have charged properly overnight. It went dead at the end of the day, but I didn't think it was a big deal. I came home and you two weren't here, and the car was gone and then I plugged my phone in and saw your missed calls. Oh, Annie, I'm so sorry."

The doctor raised his eyebrows at me, a less than subtle sign to wrap the conversation up. "It's alright, Jack, it happens, but I have to go," I said into the mobile. "Just come to the same place you picked us up last time." "Last time" was when I'd been released after giving birth to Lexie. Even though we'd been given the all-clear, it felt so surreal to be here for such a different reason now.

By the time the doctor had given me a clean bill of health, signed the discharge papers and said we could leave I only had to wait a few minutes for Jack, but I got lost in my head again.

I thought about when Mum had broken her arm a few years earlier, how Dad had waited by her side at the hospital. Or when Aria had had a vomiting bug for days, and John sat with Carrie and told her stupid jokes to stop her worrying while their daughter got an IV. The problem with Jack's phone was just bad timing, and could have happened to anyone. There was no guarantee that having a romantic partner meant there would always be someone there for you. And still, I was the single one, and I was the one who'd ended up waiting at the hospital, alone. I knew I was just feeling sorry for myself, but I felt like I had earned the right to do so. It had been a hell of a day.

When Jack pulled up to the hospital he leapt out of the car as if he were on fire. "My girls!" he cried, rushing over to throw his arms around both of us at once. I melted into him, holding him tight. Maybe I wasn't so alone, after all.

"YOU'RE STILL IN SHOCK," Jack said on the drive home, and I nodded wordlessly. He'd tried to talk like we normally would at the start of the drive, but he wasn't getting much out of me, so we'd driven in silence for several minutes.

"Are you sure you didn't need to stay overnight...?"

"No," I said quickly. "God, that's the last thing I need." I shuddered at the thought of sleeping at the hospital. "I just need some sugar or something and I'll be fine."

There was another silence, which I broke by saying something I didn't even know I was thinking. "Do you hate me?"

"What?" Jack gave an incredulous laugh. "Of course not! Why?"

I shrugged, looking down. "I thought you might blame me for the accident."

"It wasn't your fault," Jack said reasonably. "And accidents happen – that's why they call them accidents! It could have been anyone driving the car and it still would have happened."

I nodded, wondering if I would be as generous if Jack had been the one driving the car. I wanted to think I would be reasonable, but my maternal instincts might disagree. I hated myself for letting any harm come to Lexie, and could only imagine how I'd have felt if the situation was reversed.

"The pram's in the boot," I said suddenly, and Jack looked confused. "Pardon?"

"I left the pram in the boot of my car," I sighed. "I didn't think of it."

Jack laughed. "You probably had enough to think about. The pram might be kaput, now, anyway. We can get another one."

"I'll have to take tomorrow off to look after her," I added, my thoughts spiralling.

"You can if you need it for yourself, but I can take a couple of days off to look after Lexie. You've just started back, after all," he pointed out, and I nodded. I didn't want to leave Lexie ever again, but he was probably right. Going to work would be better for my mental health than sitting at home reliving the accident, anyway. I was glad Lexie was still so young. She would most likely bounce back from the accident much faster than I would.

Our first priority when we got home was to feed Lexie and put her to bed as soon as we could, since she'd had such a long day. While I was putting her down Jack ordered pizza for the rest of us, saying that we'd 'earned it'. Even Nathan seemed entirely sympathetic towards me following the accident, refilling my drink and asking all the right questions. I wondered if we could continue this newfound camaraderie without requiring me to get into a car accident regularly.

# Chapter 50

At the mothers' group catch up the following week, I filled them all in on the accident. I tried to make the story as light as possible – "the craziest thing happened on my way home!" – rather than an overdramatic plea for attention, but they still gasped in horror when I told them about it.

"That sounds like a *nightmare!*" a woman called Amy cried sympathetically, reaching out for her own son as if to stop something like that ever happening to him.

"It really wasn't that bad," I said, trying to downplay it. "I probably overreacted."

Sarah shook her head. "I've been in an accident before. They're scary enough when you're by yourself. I can't imagine how awful it must have been with Lexie there."

"I saw your glass," Erica said, wide-eyed, and we all turned to look at her. "On the road, I mean," she added. "When I was leaving, I saw the glass, and thought *thank God I missed that accident.*" There was a pause, and then the rest of us all burst out laughing. I knew she meant well, but it wasn't the most tactful comment, and her sombre delivery made it seem somehow hilarious. Erica waited a beat, looking surprised, then joined us in our laughter.

"You should have called!" Sarah exclaimed when we'd all settled down. "I work five minutes from the hospital. I could have come to you." She reached out and put an arm around me. It was a more tender gesture than I was used to from someone I didn't know well, but I appreciated it.

I thought back to the hospital, to how small and alone I had felt as I waited with Lexie. I couldn't turn back time, but just knowing Sarah would have been there for me made me feel instantly lighter. Every so often I let my single status get the better of me, but just as often, the world reminded me that I had more people in my corner than I thought.

The conversation turned more light-hearted after that, as we watched the kids playing together. I struck up a conversation with Amy, who I hadn't really spoken to the week before, and Sarah soon joined in. The three of us seemed to have a lot in common.

"How's school going?" Sarah asked after a small lull in conversation.

"Three weeks left!" I laughed, raising my fist victoriously. "I know I only work two days a week but bloody hell, it's been a challenge. I'm looking forward to having some time off."

"Then full-time next year?" Amy asked, and I nodded my confirmation. I still wasn't sure how I'd manage, but at least the part-time stint had given me a confidence boost that it was possible to juggle Lexie and work, even if it was tough at times.

"Six weeks off before I have to worry about that, though," I added. Amy shook her head enviously. "I'd love those holidays, but I couldn't do the job the rest of the time. Do you think anyone will just give me the holidays without worrying about the work?"

We laughed together. When people heard about my job they normally carried on about how I must love all the holidays without pausing to consider how tough the job could be the rest of the time, so it was nice to have Amy acknowledge that.

The three of us kept chatting as the afternoon went on, and before we left Sarah and I had arranged a playdate just for our two, away from the rest of the group. It was so hard making new friends as an adult, but having kids of a similar age seemed to be a natural way to bond.

THE LAST DAY OF TERM felt like it took an eternity to roll around, while at the same time coming in a blur. Carrie, Georgia and I had vowed to make the most of our last term together, and we had an after-school coffee break once a week, which was no mean feat considering how hectic Term 4 always gets. The struggle of getting accustomed to the workforce again, even at only a couple of days a week, meant the days often dragged, but at the same time I wished I could slow time down. I had no doubt that Carrie and I would stay in touch into the future – we were like family now, not just colleagues – but we'd worked together for our entire teaching careers. I wasn't ready to say goodbye to that.

On our last day we all dressed up a little more, ready for our Christmas party that evening. I had bought a new dress for the occasion, since so few of mine fitted now. I really had to work on that! I even went to the effort of curling my hair for the first time since becoming a mum. I had to wake up half an hour earlier, but I couldn't deny it felt good to make a bit of extra effort.

I drove into school, singing along with the radio both loudly and off-key. The end of the school year always made me feel sentimental and today was no exception, even though I'd only worked a grand total of twenty days over the year. I thought back to the last Christmas party I'd attended, laughing a little to myself as I remembered Felicia and her probing questions. I'd been agitated by her over-the-top nature, but after the roller coaster of emotions I'd been on in the year since I couldn't remember why I'd even cared about her opinion. It felt like everything in my world had changed, and the fact that it was Carrie's last day only emphasised that.

I had agreed to be the designated driver for the evening, so I picked Carrie and Georgia up on my way to school. "Last day, bitches!" Georgia crowed as she jumped into the car.

"Don't remind me," Carrie moaned. "I feel sick. I've made a huge mistake. Can I stay?" She did look a little pale. I reminded myself that as hard as it was for me to say goodbye, it had to be worse for her. I felt frustrated sometimes with the way things worked at Fallen Oaks, but I couldn't imagine leaving. Carrie had built up a fantastic reputation as a teacher and a hard worker at our school, and now she would have to go and do that all again at her new workplace. I thought about how Nathan had accused me of making it all about me, and I vowed to make an extra effort not to do that today. Today was Carrie's day.

"No more Fallen Oaks Drinking Game for you," Georgia said in a mock-sombre tone, instantly lightening the mood. "You'll have to come up with some crappy new St Catherine's Drinking Game with your crappy new work friends."

I laughed. "Your crappy new work friends will probably be all *serious* and only want to talk about *pedagogy*," I said in a sneering tone. "You'll try to come up with a drinking game with them and they'll say *oh Carrie, it's all about the children, remember.*"

"There's no way anyone there will be as much fun as we are," Georgia agreed. "No one ever is."

"You guys are great friends," Carrie grumbled. "I tell you I'm worried about my new job and you both start telling me how crappy it will be."

We giggled, Georgia and I both knowing her well enough to realise she wasn't really upset with us. "That's what friends are for," I said.

"Sarcasm is how I deal with heartbreak," Georgia added, leaning forward to put her arms around Carrie from behind. "We're going to miss this little girl *so much!*" she added, her voice sounding more suited to be talking to Alexis than to Carrie. Carrie laughed, squirming out of her grasp. "What have we told you about keeping your hands and feet to yourself?" she demanded. Georgia was deeply into love languages, and had discovered, to no one's surprise, that hers was physical touch. She reminded us of this regularly, claiming that it gave her the right to 'grope' us whenever she wanted. We often reminded her that that reasoning wouldn't hold up under the workplace sexual harassment policy.

"Anyway," Carrie added when Georgia's hands were safely back where they belonged, "I'm going to miss you guys more. At least you'll still have each other. I'll be stuck meeting new people! You know how much I hate new people." It was true. The three of us seemed loud and confident, but we were all pretty content with our existing friends. There was nothing Carrie hated more than going to a party where she didn't know anyone. I could only imagine how difficult the idea of branching out with her workplace would be for her. At least she was somewhat familiar with a few of the teachers by being a parent at the school, but working there would still be a big adjustment for her.

"Well, we just have to make a pact to catch up as often as we can outside of school," I said, trying to stop us getting too moody. "And of course, we've always got The Threesome." Our group chat was always busy even with seeing each other at work; I had no doubt the messages would be coming thick and fast with some added distance between us. I smiled wistfully at my two best girlfriends as we drove into the school parking lot for the last time together.

# Chapter 51

Holidays were always welcome, particularly the long Christmas break, but this time they came with a downside: more time with Nathan. Although I'd only been working two days a week this term, it gave us a little breathing room. My holiday pay was negligible after my small amount of working days accrued, and I didn't like going out with Lexie too often anyway because she would get too worn out, so I was spending more time around the house just out of necessity. Jack was always willing to give me some extra cash when needed, of course, especially when it came to his daughter, but I didn't want to take advantage of the arrangement. I would use his money to put food on the table, not to go out during the week. I was fine with staying home more, except that Nathan's irregular hospital schedule meant a not insignificant amount of time was spent with just the two of us and Alexis at home together during the day. I didn't love the new circumstances, but I made the best of them, busying myself with making preparations for Alexis' first Christmas. We were going to host my parents, Julie and Jack's mum here on the day. Nathan didn't see much of his family, which meant they weren't joining us, but it also meant he would be around on the day itself. I decided to make a concerted effort not to let that bother me. The day was going to be magical.

I bought a few toys, some clothes and picture books for Lexie for Christmas, but what I was most excited about was a project Mum and I were working on. I went over to her place a couple of days a week and during Lexie's naptime the two of us worked together on a quilt for Lexie for Christmas. Well, Mum did most of the work – I'd never been too crafty – but I enjoyed learning a bit more about quilting, and the quality time with Mum felt pretty special. I wished I'd done more of this before Lexie came along. I hoped my own daughter and I would manage not to drift apart the way Mum and I had for a while.

"How are things going at home?" Mum asked one day during one of our quilting sessions.

I paused, thinking the question over before responding. "Yeah, they're alright," I said. "I mean, things are great with Jack. Co-parenting with him has been easier than I thought it might be. We're on the same page for most things." Since our talk after Georgia's Mum's funeral, things had been better. Of course, we'd still had our conflicts, but we'd become a lot better at handling them now. The arguments we did have now were mostly the result of fights I'd had with Nathan, rather than actual disagreements about how to raise our daughter. I filled Mum in a bit on the situation with Nathan. "It goes beyond the living situation," I said sadly. "I just think neither of us actually likes the other as a person. I don't know how to keep going like this."

Mum patted my hand sympathetically. "I think you just have to keep putting one foot in front of the other," she said. "I know it's not easy, but if Jack's really committed to this guy then you have to do what's best for you and for Lexie. If that's living with Jack, you need to find a way to make things work with Nathan. If it's living with Lexie alone, and having joint custody with Jack, then that can work, too." I was shaking my head before she even finished her sentence. "That's not an option," I replied, and Mum nodded. "Then make it work," she said, firmly and simply.

Mum was right, and I knew it. I could wish Nathan away as much as possible, but it wouldn't make it happen. If living with Jack was a non-negotiable for me, then living with Nathan was something I would have to learn to cope with.

EVERYTHING SEEMED TO go smoothly, right up until two days before Christmas. I've always thought that people go a little crazy as they get close to Christmas, and this year was no exception. I was sitting on the floor beside the tree, legs sprawled out, wrapping Lexie's gifts after putting her to bed. It was a hot, sticky evening, so we had the air conditioning pumping. Jack was in the kitchen, humming cheerfully as he stacked the dishwasher. He'd finished work for the year that day and was in a particularly good mood, given the stress he'd been under lately with his job. From the moment Nathan walked through the front door, I could tell something was wrong.

"Well, isn't this a cosy, domestic scene," he griped, looking at us.

I raised my eyebrows. "Problem?" I asked mildly, my casual tone belying the fact that my heart rate had accelerated at his words.

Nathan smirked. "I'm just thinking how much nicer it would have been for you if I hadn't come home."

"Well, you're not exactly making it a bed of roses," I muttered.

"Calm down," Jack said to Nathan quietly, his good mood seeming to evaporate instantly. "I don't get your issue today." I tended to agree. Nathan could be easily agitated, but this particular bad mood seemed to come out of nowhere. Neither Jack nor I had done anything out of the ordinary. We hadn't even said a word before Nathan had started in on us.

Nathan gestured around the room. "You, cleaning the kitchen while the little wife wraps gifts by the tree. I can see I'm not needed here." With that, he stalked out of the room.

Jack and I stared, stunned, after him. I could see the stress on Jack's face, the toll all this was taking on him. "I'm sorry...?" I eventually uttered, knowing it sounded more like a question than an apology. Mainly because I had absolutely no clue what the hell had just happened.

Jack shook his head, obviously agreeing with me. "There's no need to be sorry. This one's completely on him." He paused, then sighed and went to move. "I guess I should follow him." He shrugged and walked away, looking lost.

I kept wrapping gifts on the floor silently, but my previously cheerful, festive mood was gone. This was proof I'd been right to dread Nathan's presence on Christmas Day. We hadn't even made it to the day yet and already he was ruining things with his tantrums.

It was nearly an hour before I heard footsteps entering the room. I turned, expecting to see Jack, but Nathan was standing there, looking sheepish.

"I'm sorry," he muttered, more to his feet than to me. It was clear he wasn't accustomed to apologising to anyone.

I gathered my thoughts before I replied. "What did I do?"

Nathan sighed. "You didn't do anything. It was me. I had a hell of a day." He came and sat down on the couch in front of me. "I just talked it over with Jack and I know it wasn't right to take it out on you guys. Basically, I had a patient die today." I nodded. It was sad, but it wasn't exactly unexpected in his line of work. I waited to hear the rest of the story.

Nathan took a deep breath. "He was a gay man, but he and his partner had spent most of their lives in the closet, and the family didn't accept it. He was an older man, you see, in his seventies." He paused. "He had adult kids, grandkids. They didn't know about the partner until six months ago."

"That's awful," I murmured.

"They wouldn't even let his partner into the room," Nathan sighed. "I mean, he had a right to be there. Legally, the hospital would have allowed him in without their approval. But he just... gave in. He seemed so broken. So resigned. They'd been together for over twenty years, and he wasn't with his partner when he died. I guess it hit a little too close to home."

I thought about this for a moment. "So then you came home and saw us."

"I saw a part of Jack's life that I'm not really a part of." Nathan ran a hand through his hair, still looking anywhere but at me. "I know that's stupid because I live with you guys, but it's how I feel. Lexie wasn't even there and it just looked so domestic. I could see this perfect little couple, and all of a sudden, I didn't seem needed."

For the first time, my heart went out to him. It was the first time Nathan had let himself be vulnerable in front of me. I had never really understood what Jack saw in him, but this was the side of Nathan that I didn't get to see much of. I hated to admit it, but from the moment I'd first heard of Nathan I'd seen him as an inconvenience, a barrier to the home situation I really wanted to have. I'd spent so long thinking of how hard it was on me having Nathan move in with us, how it had destroyed the idea of the perfect family I'd had in my head, that I'd never really thought of how difficult it must sometimes be for Nathan.

"I'm so sorry," I said, and I think he knew I wasn't just talking about the situation in the hospital today.

"I was out of line," Nathan said, "and I'm embarrassed about the way I carried on. But I guess I've been feeling insecure for a while, so today hit a little bit harder than it normally would have."

There was silence for a few minutes, which I eventually broke. "I know I can be hard work to live with sometimes," I admitted. "But I'm a good friend, Nathan, I really am. I'm a good friend to Jack. There's no reason why we can't get along, too."

He nodded. "I think we can, too. At least enough to make all of this work." I thought of how anxious I'd been, wondering if Jack would choose Nathan over me, and I realised Nathan must have been secretly concerned about the same thing.

"On one condition," I added. I closed my eyes before I went on. It wouldn't be easy, but I had to say it.

"You have to get over the idea that I'm in love with Jack. I know you think it's true, but I'm not. Yeah, once upon a time I thought there might have been something there, but I'm not the same person I was then. I would have travelled to the ends of the earth for him then. And now?" I paused. "Now, there are days when I can't stand the sight of him. Days when I just need a little bit of alone time, away from him, away from everyone. And that's okay. Actually, I think it's better this way." It was true. There was a part of me that wished I still adored Jack utterly and completely, the way I had when we first met, but our friendship was so much more real now. I was an entirely different person to the younger girl who'd fallen for him.

Nathan looked at me for the first time since he'd come back into the room, and he smiled. It was a genuine smile, the type I didn't often get from him. "I actually don't think you're in love with him," he said, with a short laugh. "I just get paranoid sometimes. I've never had a friendship like you guys do, so I guess I can't really understand it. But I'll stop questioning it."

I returned his smile. "Okay, cool. Sounds like a deal to me." I stood up from my spot on the floor and went over to the couch. I was planning to shake his hand to cement our deal, but I think I took us both by surprise by wrapping my arms around him instead. We'd never hugged before, but he held me back. As I stepped back from the hug, I saw Jack standing by the doorway, holding Alexis. He was smiling. They both were.

# Chapter 52

Christmas Day was every bit as magical as I'd hoped. I'd always held on to my childlike love for Christmas, but now that I had an infant of my own it was all the more special. Mum, Dad and Jack's mum Heather came over around ten and started showering Alexis with presents. As well as their gifts for Jack and me, Mum and Dad had bought a couple of things for Nathan, which he seemed touched by. It couldn't be easy, not having family of your own on Christmas Day.

Julie came and joined us for lunch, having spent the morning with Sidney, the man she'd gone on a first date with the evening Alexis and I had our car accident. We hadn't met him yet, but she seemed pretty smitten. I wondered if this would last.

We had a casual lunch, as was tradition in my family – given Julie's veganism and Mum wanting to relax and enjoy Christmas Day herself, we'd never gone for a traditional roast. Jack had been slightly horrified by the idea but eventually came around to serving up cold meat, salad and lasagne, as well as potato gems for Dad and me, the big kids of the family. It was a strange concoction, but we all loved it. In my opinion it was tastier than a roast, and it was far more weather-appropriate than a hot roast meal with all the trimmings. I did serve plum pudding and custard for dessert, my one nod to the tradition of the season.

After lunch we put on some Christmas songs and cracked open some more wine, then lay around chatting as we waited for our food to digest. Lexie was playing with her new toys, banging loudly on her new drum while yelling "bang! Bang!" The drum was from Julie, the classic gift of the childfree aunt who would receive no karmic payback for the torture she had enlisted on the parents. Nathan went over to play with Alexis on the floor. I saw him wince slightly at the noise, but I had to give him points for trying. It was more than he'd done before.

I smiled as I rested my head back on the couch, taking in the scene. Mum and Dad were sitting side by side, Dad humming along softly to "Have Yourself a Merry Little Christmas". Julie went and joined Nathan on the floor, and they giggled together at Lexie's symphony. The two seemed to be bonding, an unexpected friendship.

I wasn't naïve enough to think that it would all be roses from there on in – I knew Nathan and I would continue to have our issues here and there, and that I would still get a pang of loneliness from time to time if I didn't meet someone. Jack and I would no doubt fight over the choice of school for Lexie, or over when she should be allowed to start dating. But no family was perfect. No life was perfect.

It didn't have to be perfect, I thought contentedly, looking around at the house, so full of love. It was enough.

# Epilogue: Ten Years Later

A<sup></sup>*lexis*

"Happy birthday, Alexis!" Mum sang out, lighting the candles on my birthday cake and smiling widely at me.

"Legs eleven!" Dad added, wrapping his arms around me. "I remember turning eleven. I felt so grown up."

"Well, *that* was certainly a long time ago," Mum laughed, and I giggled. I love it when Mum and Dad tease each other.

"Happy birthday, Lexie," Aria exclaimed, giving me a big hug. Aria and I have always been good friends, even though she's 15 now. She wants to be a teacher when she finishes school, just like our mums, and like Aunty Georgia was before she became a vice principal. Mum has always said that Aria and I are more like cousins than friends.

I took a deep breath and blew out all the candles on my cake. "Did you make a wish?" Dad asked. "Was it something about a *boy?*"

"Dad!" I groaned. I shook my head sadly at my dad, pretending to be more embarrassed by him than I was. My Dad makes some goofy jokes sometimes, but he's actually a pretty cool guy – for someone old, anyway.

Pa came up and took the cake. "I'll cut it," he said, and Dad thanked him and put his hand on Pa's back. Pa is my Dad's husband. His real name is Luke, but when they got married four years ago, I started calling him Pa. I love my Pa almost as much as my Mum and Dad. A few kids at school think it's funny that I have two dads, but I just think I'm lucky. Dad pointed out that if Mum got married again, I would have *three* dads. She's single, though. I don't think she'll get married soon. She loves Pa though, and she always says she doesn't need a husband because she has the two best husbands already. She's not actually married to Dad or Pa, though, so that's a bit of a weird thing to say.

"I want some!" Flynn yelled, running up.

I rolled my eyes. "Wait your turn, Flynny," I told him. "Pa's still cutting it." Flynn sighed in an exaggerated way and sat down at the table, waiting for some cake. Ethan sat down beside him. Flynn and Ethan are best friends. Mum and Aunty Carrie were both pregnant with them at the same time, and they were born only two weeks apart. I like Ethan – a lot better than his older brother Lachlan anyway, who only cares about his girlfriend. I like Aria the most, of course. Jasper was there too with his mum, Sarah. Jasper and I have been friends since before I can remember. Mum and Sarah always show us these horrible photos of us playing together when we were little. There's even one of me kissing Jasper when I was, like, one! I don't remember *that* at all. Pretty gross.

Pa returned with the cake, which he'd cut neatly into pieces. Pa also made the cake – he's a baker and his cakes are amazing. He asked me what I wanted and I asked for vanilla with buttercream frosting. He made it just like I asked, but surprised me by turning the cake into a unicorn's head, with a white chocolate horn. It was amazing.

Mum has always called Flynn her mini-Jack and me her mini-me. I asked her if that meant she loved me more than Flynn and she laughed and said "no, because I love your daddy so much". It's true that Flynn looks just like Dad, but his personality is also like him. He's pretty smart and funny, just like Dad, and he's also sort of sweet, as far as little brothers go. Dad says Flynn is "kind-hearted". I think Dad is kind-hearted, too.

Dad used to date a man named Nathan. I barely remember him – I was only three when he left – but a while after that, Mum and Dad decided to have another baby and that's how we got Flynn. A couple of years ago, Mum told me all about how babies are made. *Gross!* She said they made Flynn and me differently, though. I was very glad to hear that.

I never really knew my family was different to other families until I went to school, but I didn't mind when I found out. I just felt lucky to have my family. A lot of kids' parents don't live together. Dad and Pa live just in our backyard. They call it a Granny Flat, but no Grandmas live there. Dad and Pa spend all their time in the main house, anyway, except to sleep and sometimes to have breakfast. I asked Dad once why they didn't just live in the big house with the rest of us and he said there were too many people in the house. We all have dinner together there each night, though, and that doesn't feel like too many people. Anyway, when they built the Granny Flat, they also added a pool, so it all worked out okay. Sometimes I like to sleep on a mattress on the floor in the Granny Flat. It's like camping out, but without all the mosquitos.

Grandma and Nana were at my party, too. Grandad died three years ago. I still miss him, especially on days like this, and I know Mum does too – I caught her staring at his framed photo on the wall when she didn't know I was looking. I loved having my grandmothers around, though. We see a lot of each other, and Grandma always has me for sleepovers during the holidays. She only lives ten minutes away from us, but it always makes me feel special, especially since she has Flynn over on different nights. Mum sees a lot of Grandma. She always told me that I brought her and Grandma closer together. She said they didn't see so much of each other before I was born. That makes me feel pretty special, too.

"I want the horn," Aunty Julie said, pointing at the cake. "The horn is all for the birthday girl," Mum laughed, giving her sister a little shove. Seeing Mum and Aunty Julie together sometimes made me want a sister, but for the most part I was pretty happy with my little brother.

Aunty Laura, Aunty Julie's girlfriend, smiled and wrapped her arms around Julie. "No horn for you," she said, and they both laughed. When Aunty Julie met Laura a few years ago, Mum was really surprised, but I don't know why. They seem like a pretty good couple to me. They even have their own personal training business together.

Pa started passing around pieces of cake, giving the biggest one – and the horn! – to me. I tucked in eagerly. A hand reached around to take the horn off my plate, but I smacked it away, then looked up and laughed. It was Uncle Oliver, Aunty Georgia's husband. Uncle Oliver is hilarious. He and Georgia don't have any kids together – Oliver has two of his own and Georgia has Michael, who's really old – but he's always happy to joke around with Flynn and me, and with Aunty Carrie's kids. He's really smart, too. He works at a *university*. I once heard Mum call him 'the man Georgia deserves', whatever that means. Aunty Georgia is pretty funny too, and she and Uncle Ollie are always smiling at each other and hugging and kissing. It's a bit gross, but kind of nice.

Mum's phone dinged and I saw her grab it quickly and check the message, smiling when she saw what it said. I wondered if it was a birthday message for me, but most of the people I loved were here.

"Message from Samuel?" Dad asked Mum. It sounded like he was trying to be quiet, but he wasn't really. His eyebrows were raised, and he was making a funny sort of face. Mum laughed and smacked him lightly on the arm, muttering something about "early days yet".

After dessert, we played Musical Chairs, which Ethan won. Dad suggested we play another game, but I was happy just to keep playing the music from Musical Chairs. Dad grabbed me and we started to dance around the backyard to the music with our hands together. He gave me a twirl and I spun around in a dizzy circle, then came back to Dad. Flynn ran up to join in the fun and Mum grabbed his hands and danced with him, too. When the song was over, Dad told the four of us to all link arms and we all took a big, deep bow together while the other guests clapped, cheered and Pa grinned and snapped some photos. I smiled, knowing it was a moment I was going to remember forever. My eleventh birthday, with all my family.

# ACKNOWLEDGEMENTS

I have to start off by thanking my sister and fellow author, Gemma Johns, for being my first reader and answering all of my questions about writing and publishing (and there were a lot of them!) Gemma, I'm not sure I could have got this far without you, and I can't thank you enough.

I also owe my thanks to the rest of my family, particularly my sister Melanie, my parents and my ten nieces and nephews, who are always such a source of love and support for me.

One niece in particular requires a special shout out – Anastasia, from Studio Yves, for doing such a fantastic job with my cover and for patiently responding to all of my requests for revisions because I didn't really know what I was after. Anastasia, thank you for your time and patience!

I have talked my friends' ears off about my writing for the past year, so I owe them all a debt of gratitude for listening patiently and encouraging me that I really could do this.

I started this book years ago, but shelved it because I couldn't figure out what it was missing. Finally, it came to me - every educator needs a teacher squad behind them, and Annie is no exception. So thank you to Kylie and Rachael, my real-life Carrie and Georgia, for the laughter, the stories and the Threesome chat.

Finally, thank you to my readers! I hope that you've enjoyed reading about Annie and Jack as much as I enjoyed writing about them.

# About the Author

Larissa Johns always loved writing and grew up dreaming of becoming a published author. She celebrated her love of writing through completing a journalism degree, but soon found it was not the right fit for her. Larissa decided to pursue a career in education instead, and has now worked as a primary school teacher in Brisbane for over ten years.

In her spare time Larissa loves all types of pop culture, including reading, music and far too many trips to the cinemas. She also devotes herself to spoiling her pet cavoodle, Indiana Johns. Larissa does not wish to have a baby with any of her gay friends.